D1413155

THE HIDDEN TRUTH

Other books by Michael Senuta:

Matt Train
Incident at Copper Creek
The Vengeance Brand

THE HIDDEN TRUTH

•

Michael Senuta

AVALON BOOKS
NEW YORK

Published by Thomas Bouregy & Co., Inc.
160 Madison Avenue, New York, NY 10016

Library of Congress Cataloging-in-Publication Data

Senuta, Michael.
    The hidden truth / Michael Senuta.
        p. cm.
    ISBN 978-0-8034-9970-6 (hardcover : acid-free paper)
1. Robbery investigation—Fiction.   2. Montana—Fiction.   I. Title.

    PS3569.E63H53 2009
    813'.54—dc22

                                          2009004417

PRINTED IN THE UNITED STATES OF AMERICA
ON ACID-FREE PAPER
BY HADDON CRAFTSMEN, BLOOMSBURG, PENNSYLVANIA

To my parents, William and Cathyrnne

Chapter One

Will Grant shifted his feet uneasily as he stood on the platform near the ticket office. The Montana sky was heavy with clouds, foretelling a coming snow. A cold snap had gripped the area for days. The air was laden with moisture, and the ground was as hard as iron. Grant, however, seemed unaffected by the temperature despite the fact that he possessed no outer coat. His ill-fitting suit was his only protection against a thermometer that registered ten degrees and continued to plummet. He felt awkward as he stood alone, his arms held stiffly at his sides. He thought that the ticket master had regarded him with disdain as money had passed between them. Perhaps it had been his imagination. Ordinarily, he was not a self-conscious man, but then the last year of his life had been anything but ordinary.

A shrill whistle pierced the still morning air, and Grant gazed into the distance, where he sighted a thin spire of white smoke that hung briefly in the air before dissolving against a backdrop of mountains. The locomotive moved closer into view, black and gray, as it wormed its way across the ground, behemoth-like, before shedding its otherworldly appearance and transforming itself into the tons of recognizable manmade metal that gave one a more comfortable feeling.

There were few passengers ready to board. Unlike Grant, they had chosen to sit in the warmth of the depot, but now they emerged like rabbits from their holes, bundled from chins to knees in their heavy coats—a woman and her little girl, a drummer carrying his sample case, a business-type puffing a long cheroot. They congregated in a small knot near the edge of the platform, watching the train as it made its slow arrival amidst a flurry of metallic noises, jets of steam, and smoke. It chugged its way forward grudgingly, until it ground to a stop parallel to the platform with a precision of movement that defied its enormous bulk.

In a moment, the conductor emerged from one of the passenger cars, placed a footstool on the platform, and descended. He greeted the circle of travelers, assisted the woman and her child up the steps, and then strolled over to the depot, where he disappeared inside. In the meantime, water was taken on from a tank, and an engineer appeared, carrying an oil can. He strolled alongside the train, lubricating one thing or another, inspecting various parts of machinery until he appeared to be satisfied that everything was in working order before returning to his position at the front of the train.

The platform was empty now, and Grant made his way to the train. He had a smooth stride and was light on his feet. He was nearly six feet tall, lean, and broad-shouldered. His face might be described as handsome but for a scar that extended for an inch just above his left cheekbone. He entered the passenger car, which was occupied by only the four who had just boarded. They sat near the front of the car, near the stove. The woman eyed him narrowly and whispered something to her daughter, who glanced up at Grant. The others turned, regarded him for a moment without expression and then looked away. Grant slipped into the last seat of the car, pulled down his Stetson, and lowered his head.

Twenty minutes later, the train lurched slightly as the wheels turned and a slow, steady momentum was attained. They passed the platform, left the depot behind, and were soon cutting across the open prairie. Grant remained ensconced in the corner of his seat. He could hear light banter from the other passengers, but he averted glancing in their direction. Finally, he raised his Stetson and concentrated on the view from the window. Flat terrain stretched for miles before it gave way to rolling hills and mountains in the far distance. He had not seen such open land for a long time, and he could not help but appreciate its beauty and scope. In fact, he could not take his eyes off the view, so mesmerized was he by the expanse and wealth of the land. He did not even hear the conductor approach and ask for his ticket. A tap on his shoulder was necessary to rouse him from his reverie. He looked up and heard the conductor repeat his request. Grant reached into his pocket and surrendered the ticket. The conductor punched it and returned it, seeming to scrutinize Grant's appearance coolly before moving down the aisle. Grant shrugged and once again stared out the window.

Within an hour, snow started to fall. It came in pinpoint crystals at first, and then it changed to thick, fluffy flakes—millions and millions that filled the air and covered the ground with an ermine coat. Evergreens that dotted the foothills quickly lost their identity, submitting to the white veil that touched everything in sight. The flakes began to cling and accumulate on the windows until tiny geometric patterns formed on the panes like, and yet unlike, any other. Grant found himself alternating his stare from the foothills to the pane just a few inches from his eyes. Both held an equal fascination for him.

Soon, the little girl was leaning against her mother, her eyelids heavy, her drowsiness enhanced by the rhythmic sway of the train. The businessman lit his cigar and smoke began to drift through the car. He and the drummer sat together and opened a deck of cards. Their occasional comments were the only sounds in the car that reminded Grant that he was not alone.

In time, the conductor made his way down the aisle with a tray of sandwiches and coffee. Grant declined the food but accepted the coffee. He took a swallow. It was hot and strong, and it went down smoothly. It felt good when it hit his stomach. He cradled the tin cup in both hands. It warmed his fingers, and it took his mind off the snow and the cold. He knew, however, that there would be more cold ahead.

When the train made its next stop, the woman and her child and the drummer departed. They picked up speed again, leaving behind the snow-covered roofs of the small town. In minutes, the train began to climb as the mountains loomed closer. The tracks followed a circuitous path now that disappeared among the trees and boulders ahead. The businessman eyed Grant from his seat on the far side of the car. Slowly, he rose to his feet, stretched, and then sauntered down the aisle. When he reached Grant's seat, he paused and regarded Grant closely. "You in the mood for a friendly game of poker?"

Grant shook his head.

The man was short but wide through the chest and stomach. He wore a blue pinstriped suit. A gold watch fob dangled from his vest pocket. His face was ruddy and his grin revealed a row of uneven teeth. "Oh, come now, we've got another two hours before the next stop. I never like to pass the time alone when I'm traveling."

"No thanks."

The businessman took the cigar from his lips and

clutched it in his fat fingers. "No reason to be unsociable, mister. If it's a lack of money you're worried about, we can play for matchsticks."

"I'm just not interested. Maybe later."

"Well, I think you'll change your mind once you get your head in the game." He removed a deck of cards from his coat pocket and started to move toward the seat across from Grant.

Grant raised his leg and dropped it on the cushion opposite him, effectively blocking the businessman from sitting down.

The businessman glared down at Grant. The corners of his mouth tightened. "Look here, mister, I don't need any jailbird givin' me the cold shoulder. If that's the way you want to play it, it's fine by me." He shoved the cigar back into his mouth and turned away in a huff. Grant watched him as he waddled down the aisle, shoved his way past the conductor, and plopped into one of the seats at the far side of the car.

The conductor, who had witnessed the scene, moved up to Grant. He glanced over his shoulder at the businessman, who was now sending thick clouds of smoke into the air as if he were on fire. "Sorry about that."

Grant shrugged. "Does it show that much . . . that I'm an ex-convict, that is?"

The conductor smiled. "Most men who are have that look about them. You're no exception."

Grant nodded resignedly as he looked down at his suit. "The suit's part of it. There's no mistaking that, but there's more to it than that. I can't really explain it. I guess what I mean to say is that it's just the cut of a man who's been behind bars. When a man hasn't been around normal folks for a while . . . well, you can read it in his actions." The conductor grinned. "Besides, about half the men who are released from the state penitentiary board the train where you did in Clayton."

Grant smiled as he watched the conductor turn away. He stared out the window a while longer and then decided to stretch his legs. He moved to the rear of the car and stepped through the door. An icy blast of air met him as he secured the door behind him and stood next to the railing. He watched the coupling sway gently between the passenger car and the baggage car. He marveled at how a single metal rod could hold together two such large railroad cars. A simple twist and pull and one section of the train could become disconnected, left to drift along the tracks until it came to a gradual stop in the middle of the countryside. It was much like a man's life. One swift, unexpected twist and he could suddenly find himself alone . . . in the middle of nowhere.

As Grant stared at the coupling, watching it ice up before his eyes, his thoughts drifted back over the last year of his life. He still could not believe what had happened to him. The events were branded in his memory, and he knew that they would never leave him. He could do nothing to obliterate that fateful night in Coltonville, the town where he lived. He could remember walking to the express office as if it were yesterday. It was just after dark.

There were not many people on the street. Most folks had already headed for home or were having dinner. He was on his way to the express office to meet his close friend, Tom Elsworth. The two of them had planned on having a steak dinner at the Colton Cafe. Tom was scheduled to work in his office all night. Earlier in the week, he had signed for $40,000 in cash, a payroll for an engineering firm that was based in the area. Tom usually remained on guard at the express office on nights when large sums of cash or gold were on hand. He had hired a man to spell him for a few hours so that he could get some dinner and take a short nap.

Grant knew that he was a bit early and that Tom's relief would probably not be there, but he was hungry, and he was anxious to talk to his friend about a new horse he had considered buying. As Grant walked along the boardwalk, he saw that the shades were drawn over the windows of the express office, for it was Tom's routine to do so after working hours. Grant could see a soft glow of light through the shades, which told him that Tom was on duty. Grant knocked on the door, knowing that Tom would have it locked for security reasons. He waited but there was no response. He knocked again and called out to Tom. When there was still no answer, he tried the door. To his surprise, the knob turned in his hand, and he entered. In the dim light of the room, he could barely make out Tom, who was standing behind the counter. Tom's face was partly in shadow. His expression looked strange, and he did not speak. As Grant took a step forward, he heard a shot. It was loud within the small room, and he saw Tom clutch his chest and fall. He then recalled seeing a muzzle flash from a dark corner off to his right, and he felt himself drifting in darkness as if he were falling into a well.

After that, events moved quickly, and they all moved against him. He awoke in a jail cell, feeling the odd construction of a bandage over his cheekbone. The town doctor was standing beside him, speaking to him. Grant was dazed, and the words seemed muffled, garbled. He understood the doctor when he told him that he had been shot, and that the wound had only grazed him. The doctor said something about bone chips . . . cleaning sawdust from the wound . . . a possible concussion . . . the rest of his words eluded Grant. A few minutes later, Grant's focus was better and he tried to sit up. His head spun as he threw his legs over the edge of the bunk. The sheriff and his deputy were standing behind the bars, staring down at him. The sequence of events was then laid out for him by the sheriff. Grant and his confederate had conspired to rob the express office. Tom was killed in the process, and the payroll that he had been holding was stolen. The safe was open but empty of everything except some papers. A .45 was clutched in Grant's hand. Tom had been shot with a .45. Tom's own gun, a .44, was found next to his body. One shot had been discharged from it. It was assumed that Grant had killed Tom, and that Tom had grazed Grant in the shootout. A rider had been seen galloping out of town just seconds before the shots had been fired—Grant's assumed accomplice, who had presumably escaped with the payroll. Darkness had prevented a posse from forming until the following morning. By then, no sign was discovered of the rider.

Grant, of course, vehemently protested his innocence, explaining the circumstances as he knew them. His account of the events held little water, however, for there was one inexplicable fact that doomed his version of the shooting. Within seconds of hearing the gunshots, several townsmen quickly emerged from nearby buildings. In fact, a man and his wife were passing along the boardwalk just across the street from the express office at the time the shots were fired. They, along with every other witness, remained adamant about one point—no one had emerged from the express office. It was a fact that whoever had fired the shots still had to be in the office. The sheriff and his deputy arrived on the scene almost immediately. Upon finding Tom's body and Grant lying wounded, they searched the express office. They discovered that the windows were shuttered and barred. The back door was locked and bolted. There were some large wooden crates in the back room. The deputy even opened them to make certain that no one was concealed within. It was the one fact that Grant could not explain, and in the end it proved to be his downfall.

A trial was held. It was a fair trial, but Grant was found guilty of robbery and murder and was sentenced to life in the state penitentiary. There were conflicting opinions among the townsmen as to his guilt. He had not lived in Coltonville long. Most people did not really know him that well. Tom, on the other hand, had been one of the town's most popular residents. That, in itself, did not bode well. Some considered Grant's explanation reasonable—that the gun could have been fired by a third party and placed in his hand; nevertheless, in the end, his version of the events was heavily outweighed by the inescapable fact that no one could have escaped the express office after the shots had been fired. The prosecutor kept hammering away at that fact, and Grant's attorney could not get around it. Grant, himself, could not provide a satisfactory explanation. He understood the verdict, and he accepted it, for he could do nothing else.

That was the way that matters stood until about a month ago, when a man by the name of Charley Ferris came into the picture. Grant knew him from Coltonville but only slightly. Ferris had been fatally wounded in a nearby town by an unknown assailant. Before dying, he confessed to his part in the robbery of the Coltonville express office. His story was sketchy. He died, in fact, before he implicated anyone else, but in the presence of the local sheriff and other witnesses, he cleared Grant's name. An investigation was held, and the authorities concluded that the confession of a dying man carried enough weight to overturn Grant's conviction.

Now, here he was, a free man once again, returning to the town where he had been accused of murdering his best friend. He was not particularly anxious to see

Coltonville again, or the people who had sent him away, but he still owned a small spread just outside of town. It was his, and he intended to work it again. Besides, he had a score to settle with someone. Someone had killed his friend and shot him and left him to take the blame for murder and robbery. As far as he could tell, there was at least one man running free who had to answer for that. Whether or not he was still in Coltonville, Grant had no idea, but it was as good a place to start as any.

The train lurched, and Grant's concentration was splintered. Suddenly, he became more aware of the intense cold. He fastened the top button of his suit coat and pulled up his collar. The landscape was flitting by very quickly now, and the snow showed no sign of letting up. He realized that to remain outside much longer, despite his mood, would prove foolish. He abandoned the platform and returned to the warmth of the passenger car. The businessman was still sitting in the same place, playing solitaire on a tray. The air was laden with his cigar smoke, more noticeable to Grant now after he had just come in from the cold. He slipped back into his seat and once again stared out the window.

Chapter Two

The train pulled into Coltonville fifteen minutes behind schedule. Grant stepped onto the snow-covered platform and looked around. Besides the railroad personnel, he saw no one near the depot. He was not surprised, considering the weather. He cast his eyes down the street toward the town buildings. The roofs were heavily laden with snow, giving every structure a uniform appearance. He watched feathers of smoke rise from chimneys and disappear in the blanket of falling snow. There appeared to be no sign of a letup. He thought that the town seemed unusually quiet. Perhaps the activity in the streets was muffled by the snowfall.

Rounding the corner of the depot, Grant was a bit startled to see a tall figure looming before him. He halted in his tracks and stared at the man who stood on

13

the boardwalk, his hands tucked into the pockets of his sheepskin coat. Grant recognized him at once as Ken Logan, the sheriff of Coltonville.

"Welcome back, Will," Logan announced. He was a big man, six-four, two hundred thirty pounds. His eyes were narrow, his nose and chin prominent. A .45 was holstered on his right hip at an angle that suggested he was well versed in using it.

"Hello, Sheriff."

"Pleasant trip?"

Grant nodded.

"Never did like trains myself. Don't like the feeling of being cooped up. Give me a horse and an open range any day."

"You usually stand in the snow and cold and wait for trains to pull in . . . or have you been expecting me?"

Logan surrendered a small grin. "I thought you might be headed this way."

"Any reason why I shouldn't be?"

"None that I can think of. You're a free man. You still own property here. It's yours to work as you see fit."

"Then, why the reception?"

Logan drew his hands from his pockets and pulled his coat collar closer around him. "Why don't we go to my office for a cup of coffee."

Grant eyed him narrowly, but he fell in beside Logan as the lawman stepped onto the street.

There were few passersby as they made their way down the main street of Coltonville. From what Grant could tell, the town had changed little in the time he had been gone. As they stepped in front of the express office, Grant paused.

Logan noticed his hesitation. Following Grant's gaze, he said, "Your friend, Steve Collins, is working part-time for the express company now."

"I heard. His sister wrote me about it when I was in prison. Steve is a good man."

"As I recall, you were friendly with Mary before you went off to prison."

"That's old news, Sheriff."

"She's a nice girl . . . still unmarried. No reason why you can't pick up where you left off."

Grant raised an eyebrow at Logan. "Since when has matchmaking become part of your job, Sheriff?"

Logan smiled. "Let's get that coffee."

They crossed the street and stepped onto the board-walk, where Logan stomped his boots before entering his office. Grant followed him in and was met immediately with a rush of warm air. It felt good at first, but then Grant sensed that the room was uncomfortable. Logan dropped his Stetson on a wooden chair and removed his coat and hung it on a wall peg. "Sit down, Will," he said as he moved to one of the windows and raised it about a foot. "I like to keep my office hot ever since I froze my feet in that blizzard a few years back. Sometimes I forget that it's too hot for others."

"It's all right," Grant said, unbuttoning his suit coat and finding a chair. He glanced around the office. It looked exactly as he remembered it when he had last been here a year ago. It was small but neat. One wall was covered with dodgers. Another contained a rifle rack. A door led to a back room, which Grant knew contained the jail cells. A potbelly stove was positioned in one corner of the office, on which a coffeepot sat. Logan hoisted the pot and filled two cups. He handed one to Grant and then took a long swallow from the other. He sat down behind a large walnut desk covered with papers. There was a wire basket containing some correspondence off to one side.

"I've got some sugar here in my desk if you'd like some."

Grant shook his head. "Just what is it that you wanted to say to me, Sheriff?"

Logan drained the rest of his cup and placed it near the edge of his desk. He leaned back in his chair, coupled his hands and rested them across his stomach. "I just wanted to see how you felt about everything."

"Do you mean . . . am I bitter?"

"For a start, yes."

"You bet I am, but not to the point where I'd let it cloud my judgment. I had a fair trial. I don't blame the town for my conviction."

"Well, I'm relieved to hear that."

"On the other hand, I don't hold any fondness for the townsmen either. They didn't believe my story, and that tells me something about them. I also know that there's a man out there somewhere who killed my friend and took away a year of my life. That tends to make me angry, and I'm interested in finding him."

"I can understand your feelings, but that's still my job."

"And I don't plan to get in your way."

"Well, that's good—"

"As long as you don't get into mine."

Logan's face stiffened.

"I still don't know what happened that night, Sheriff, and I was a part of it. Maybe I'll never find the answers, but I intend to keep digging."

Logan digested his words carefully. He leaned forward and pushed his cup across his desk. "This Charley Ferris . . . how well did you know him?"

"I knew him when I saw him. That's about all. As I recall, he spent a lot of his time in the saloon."

"That's true enough. He was a bottle with a man wrapped around it. Maybe that's why there are so many folks who don't believe his story."

Grant smirked. "Oh, so that's it, is it? There are those who still think I'm guilty."

"That's part of it."

"And you arranged this little meeting to suggest that I might not be considered a good risk for a loan at the bank, or I may not get elected to the town council."

Logan allowed himself a smile. "Just don't expect a handshake and a friendly smile from everybody. There are those who think you should still be behind bars."

"Well, that's their problem. The people who count believe otherwise, and I'm here."

"Just thought I'd let you know. Even a free man is sometimes marked."

"As long as they don't bother me, I won't bother them."

"Well, that's just the point. I won't always be around to protect you."

"I can take care of myself."

Logan regarded him closely.

"By the way, Sheriff, just what are your feelings as to my guilt or innocence?"

"My feelings don't amount to a hill of beans. My duty is to enforce the law. The law says that you're a free man entitled to the same rights as anyone else. If someone violates your rights, I'll do whatever is necessary."

It was a straightforward enough declaration, even though Logan sidestepped answering Grant's pointed question, but in all fairness, it was as much of an answer as Grant could expect. During his arrest and trial, he often wondered about Sheriff Logan's opinion. Even though Grant could never fathom the lawman's thoughts, he had to admit that Logan had investigated his case fairly and thoroughly.

"Is there anything else, Sheriff?"

"Just one thing. I don't know if you know it or not, but that money that was stolen from the express office . . . the forty thousand dollars . . ."

"What about it?"

"It's never turned up."

The words stunned Grant, and Logan noted his surprise.

Grant took a sip of his coffee and placed the cup on the desk. "None of it?"

"Not a dollar. We've had a few folks move out of town over the last year—not the kind I would suspect of pulling off the express robbery, you understand, but I've kept track of them. There's no sign that any part of that payroll shipment ever exchanged hands anywhere, and we've circulated the serial numbers of those bills to every bank west of the Mississippi. It's almost as though they never existed."

"Somebody's been mighty patient," Grant mused.

"It looks that way . . . if he's still alive, that is."

Grant shot a questioning look at Logan.

"Well, look at it this way. The kind of people who stoop to murder and robbery aren't your usual Sunday-go-to-meetin' types. They tend to associate with others who are just as ruthless. Look at Charley Ferris, for instance. I'll wager it wasn't the local minister or the town mayor who filled him with lead . . . and if he's dead, how do we know that his accomplice isn't . . . killed by someone just like him?"

Grant shrugged. "In that case, the money may never turn up."

"It may not, but then again . . ." He extended his hands, palms upward, as if in speculation.

It was an interesting theory that Logan put forth. Grant

mulled it over. It could account for the fact that the money had never surfaced. After all, the reason why people stole money was to spend it. The only drawback to Logan's line of reasoning was that if the money were never recovered, Tom Elsworth's murderer would never be identified, and Grant would never be completely exonerated of the crime. He rose to his feet. "Thanks for the coffee."

"What are your plans?"

Grant buttoned his suit coat again. "I'm going to rent a horse at the livery and buy some supplies at the mercantile. Then, I'm riding out to my ranch."

Logan nodded. He climbed to his feet and extended his hand. "I wish you luck."

Grant hesitated and then accepted Logan's firm grip. He left the office and stood outside on the boardwalk for a minute, considering everything the sheriff had said. He then considered the man himself. He did not know exactly what to make of him. For the time being, he decided to trust him. Glancing up and down the street, he saw a single rider moving away from him. A wagon was parked near one of the stores, but there was no one about. The boardwalks and the streets were empty. It was too cold. He saw the brightly painted sign for Barrow's Livery a block away, and he immediately headed in that direction.

Grant calculated that the snow was up to his ankles as he trudged along the street. The sky was gray, and the flakes were cold against his face. He pulled his coat more closely about him and stuck his hands under his armpits. The livery door was slightly ajar, and Grant pushed against it until he was able to slip through. The odors of horses and hay immediately struck his nostrils as his eyes adjusted to the dim light offered by a pair of lanterns hanging from posts. Lud Barrow was working in the nearest stall. When he noticed Grant, he leaned his pitchfork against the wall, brushed off his hands, and stepped toward him. He was short and thin, with a ragged beard and worn clothes that looked comfortable and perfectly suited for one in his profession. As soon as he recognized Grant, his usually warm expression altered. It was obvious that he felt uncomfortable upon seeing Grant walk into his stable, perhaps because he had served on the jury that had convicted him.

"Hello, Mr. Barrow."

"Hello, Will."

There was an uneasy moment of silence before Barrow said, "I heard about your release. I reckon you're glad to be a free man again."

"You'll never know."

Barrow shifted his weight uneasily from one foot to the other. "Well, what can I do for you?"

"I need to rent a horse for a day or two."

Barrow nodded. "Help yourself."

Grant glanced through the stable and pointed at the second stall. "That bay looks all right."

"I'll saddle him for you."

If Grant had wondered exactly how Barrow was going

to react to dealing with him, his concern was dispelled. He felt further relieved when he inquired as to the cost.

"Oh, just take him. Bring him back when you're done with him."

Grant considered Barrow for a long moment. He reached into his pocket and drew out a coin, which he placed in the ostler's hand.

Leaving the livery, Grant made his way to the mercantile, which was the last building on Coltonville's main street. It was owned and operated by Red Morris and his wife, an elderly couple who were among the town's founding fathers. Grant tied the bay to a hitching rail and entered the store. Grant rubbed his hands and looked around him. The mercantile contained a cluttered collection of articles that ranged from tools, clothes, and bolts of cloth to household items, cook ware, and foodstuffs. Red Morris always seemed to know exactly where everything was, right down to the last needle and spool of thread. The old-timer emerged from the back room just as Grant approached the counter. His hair was even redder than Grant had remembered. His face was hard set, as if it were cut from wood. He spread his fingertips on the countertop and regarded Grant narrowly. He did not speak, waiting instead to be addressed.

Grant had never felt particularly comfortable around Red Morris. He felt even less so now. "Hello, Mr. Morris."

The store owner nodded but did not respond.

Grant wondered if he should bother to place his order.

He decided that he had no choice. "I need some supplies."

Morris hesitated, then picked up a pencil and a piece of paper and wrote down Grant's order as he dictated it. Grant reeled off a long list that included a pound of bacon, two pounds of coffee, a dozen eggs, a pound of sugar, a sack of flour, half a dozen tins of beans, and one tin of peaches. He then asked Morris to place it all in a sack.

Morris scurried about, grabbing items from the shelves behind him as though he wanted Grant out of his store as quickly as possible.

Grant had no desire to remain any longer than necessary. He placed some notes on the counter and collected his change—four pennies. He hefted the sack and started for the door when he noticed a jar of peppermint sticks. Reaching back into his pocket, he removed the four pennies—the last of his money. He dropped one on the counter and selected one of the sticks. He stuck it in his shirt pocket, grinned to himself, and turned for the door. Once outside, he tied the sack to his saddle horn and rode west toward his spread.

Chapter Three

Despite the cold and the snow, the ride to his ranch was the most pleasant Grant had ever taken. Seeing the open land, being free again, going home . . . the sensations were unimaginable to someone who had never done time before. The land was exactly as he had remembered it. The trees, the rocks, the rolling hills . . . he had seen them all so vividly in his dreams so many times during his imprisonment. Now, he was back again, enjoying what he had always taken for granted. When he left the main road for the side road that led to his place, his heart began to pound. Suddenly, he could not get there soon enough. He paused at the top of the rise that overlooked his spread and drank in the sight. It was his first glimpse of his ranch house and barn in over a year.

The structures were humble and looked cold and lonely under the layer of snow, but he was proud that they were his. A man needed a section of land to call his own—regardless of its size and condition. This belonged to him, and its mere existence gave him a good feeling deep inside. Memories of his land had helped to keep him sane. Now, he was finding it hard to believe that he was even looking at it again. He urged the horse onward, descending from the rise, and moving in the most direct line he could toward the ranch house.

He tied the bay to the hitching rail and stepped onto the porch. He knocked the snow off his boots and opened the door. Everything looked as he had remembered. He lit a lamp and then assessed the parlor and the kitchen more closely. Everything looked remarkably neat—not like a house that had been unattended for a year. Then, he recalled why. Mary Collins and her brother Steve had promised to maintain everything for him while he was in prison. He smiled, for the furniture appeared dusted and the rooms seemed aired.

The first thing he did was to start a fire, for the house was unbelievably cold. There was still an ample stack of firewood on the hearth, and within minutes he had a comfortable blaze going. Next, he moved into the kitchen, where he started the stove. He quickly heated some water and then washed his long unused dishes and his coffeepot. He then stepped outside and retrieved his sack of supplies. Soon, he had a hearty meal on the table—four eggs, six slices of bacon, and a full pot of coffee. He would have enjoyed some biscuits, but he was too hungry to wait. He decided he would bake some later.

He poured himself another cup of coffee and retreated to an armchair near the fireplace, where he propped up his feet and enjoyed the warmth and the pleasant aroma of the burning wood. He decided to make plans for the following day. First thing in the morning he would go into town and drop by the bank. Before being sent to prison, he had made arrangements with Herbert Morton, the local banker, to sell his cattle and all his other stock. Morton, in turn, agreed to draw the money from Grant's account in order to pay his property taxes for as long as the money held out. According to Grant's calculations, he should still have close to $2,000 left in his name. That was one positive. The other was the fact that there was no mortgage on the ranch. He would have enough to start up another herd in the spring. That was something he could consider later, but he did want to get an idea of his financial status and test the waters if he needed to borrow on his spread. He would also need some pocket money.

Next, he wanted to visit Ed Marley, his attorney, to determine if anything new had been learned about Charley Ferris. Marley had written him several times over the last month or so of his imprisonment, informing him of the developments of his case and the details concerning Ferris' sudden admission. Marley's correspondence had hinted at the possibility of his release and had served to rekindle Grant's spirits at a time when he had all but lost hope.

It was getting late. Grant drained his cup and returned to the kitchen, where he washed his dirty dishes. Next, he went outside and led the bay into the barn, where he stabled it for the night. He then returned to the house and made his way to his bedroom. There was a small stack of wood in the bin next to the fireplace. He went to work, and in no time at all the room was comfortable. He examined his bedding and then looked in his closet. Everything seemed fresh. His shirts smelled as though they had only recently been washed. There was a very agreeable odor about them that he recognized immediately. The clothes had been washed in a special soap. Slowly, a smile formed on his face, for he thought of Mary, who had to have been here quite recently. She would have heard of his impending release and, most likely, washed and cleaned everything for his convenience. He had thought about Mary often during his first few months in prison. The two of them had been friends—good friends—and they might have had a future together, but he had done his best to force her out of his thoughts once he realized that he was not likely to be released. Now, the situation had suddenly changed. He wondered how Mary felt. Surely, she must still hold him in some regard, since she returned to clean his house. On the other hand, maybe it was simply an act of kindness from one friend to another. Even now, he would have to wait and see how matters developed, for there were other problems that had to be resolved first, questions concerning his guilt that would affect his future as well as the future of anyone who might be close to him. He was tired, more tired than he realized. He removed his clothes and crawled into bed. He was asleep in minutes.

Grant rose early the next morning. A glance through the window told him that the snowfall was over and the sky was clear again. He washed and shaved and then selected a clean shirt and pants. He placed several more pieces of wood on the fire in the parlor and then started the stove. First, he made a pot of coffee. Then, he decided to bake some biscuits. No sooner had he taken out the flour than he heard the sound of a wagon approaching. He wondered who could be calling on him. He wondered how many people even knew that he had returned yet. He opened the door and was overjoyed to see Mary Collins and her brother Steve standing on the porch. Mary quickly threw her arms around him and hugged him tightly. Grant picked her up and twirled her around.

"Well, come on in! I just put on a pot of coffee," he announced.

"Oh, Will, it's so wonderful to see you again." She beamed, her large blue eyes shining brightly, her cheeks flushed from the cold. She removed her hat, revealing a mane of blond hair.

Grant took her hat and wrap and hung them on wall pegs near the door.

Steve entered after her and extended his hand.

Grant accepted it and grinned broadly at him. "Steve, my friend, how've you been?"

"Fine, Will, just fine," he said, hanging his coat next to his sister's. He grinned back at Grant, flashing a nice row of teeth. His eyes were dark and his hair was curly. His hands were strong from the woodworking he did. Mary and Steve had moved west from Kansas. They had arrived in Coltonville about six months before Grant had.

"Oh, Will, you haven't had your breakfast yet," Mary said as she glanced at the table.

"No, I was just about to make some biscuits."

"Let me. You can talk to Steve while I take care of this kitchen work."

Quickly and smoothly, she moved about, kneading the dough, setting the table, and frying the eggs while Grant and Steve sat down at the table and talked.

"Well, how's the carpentry business?"

"It's fairly good. I get enough jobs to keep me busy, but I'll never get rich with a hammer and nails."

"No, I imagine not."

"I took a part-time position at the express office."

"Mary mentioned that in one of her letters. So did Sheriff Logan when I talked to him yesterday."

"I have Tom Elsworth to thank for the job. He's the one who hired me a week or so before the robbery. The management liked my work. They kept me on for my carpentry skills and for a little clerking."

"That's something anyway."

Steve glanced around the house. "Speaking of carpentry, after you were sent away, some hooligans broke in here. Maybe they thought they'd find the payroll money here . . . I don't know. They made a mess of things. I repaired that wooden chair over there and that shelf. I also replaced the hasps on your door."

Grant expressed his surprise. "I had no idea. Thanks, Steve."

"Mary's done most of the work, though. She's been here at least once a month, cleaning and dusting. She's even tended to your clothes."

"I can tell," Grant returned, sniffing his shirt sleeve. "It smells better than the day I bought it. It has to be that sweet smelling soap you use, Mary."

"It is. It's called Marberry's, and I special order it all the way from St. Louis." She poured the coffee and placed some eggs on Grant's plate. "The biscuits will be ready shortly, but you can get started in the meantime."

"You two aren't eating?"

"No, we've already had breakfast. We'll just have coffee with you," Mary replied. She sat down beside Grant and regarded him closely.

He smiled at her. "Anything wrong, Mary?"

"No, I'm just thinking how good it is to have you back. You look the same . . . a little thinner maybe."

"I did drop a few pounds. Prison food isn't very good," he said, lifting his fork and tasting the eggs. "Mmm . . . you haven't lost your touch with a skillet."

She grinned. It was a nice grin, and he enjoyed looking at her.

"Your biscuits are ready." She got up from the table and moved to the stove, from which she pulled out a tray containing a dozen plump biscuits. She dropped them on a dish and set them before Grant.

Grant picked up one of them and broke it in half. It was hot to the touch as steam escaped the dough. He blew on it before he took a hefty bite. Rolling his eyes, he announced, "They're delicious!"

Mary shrugged him off, but it was obvious that she was pleased with the compliment.

"Well, Will, what will you do now that you're a free man? Will you start up the ranch again?" Steve asked.

Grant took a swallow of coffee between bites. "I've been thinking about it. In fact, I was planning to ride into town today. I want to talk to Herb Morton at the bank. But there's plenty of time to make any decisions about the ranch. The weather won't break for several weeks yet."

Steve nodded. "If you need anything, Mary and I have a little cash set aside."

"Thanks, Steve, but I think I'll be all right. I still have some money in the bank, and my ranch is clear."

"All you have to do is ask."

Grant placed his hands on their shoulders. "My father always said that a man who has friends has all that he'll ever need."

Mary cast a warm smile at him. "How about some more coffee, Will?"

"No thanks, Mary. I have quite a bit to do. I'm thinking of riding over to Ridley today too."

"Ridley?"

"That's where Charley Ferris was killed."

Mary and Steve exchanged a quick look.

"I thought I'd poke around . . . see if I can learn any more about him. Maybe I can come up with some leads."

Mary placed her hand on his. "Will, you're a free man now. You're out of prison, you're home again. You've got a ranch to run, a future. Why dredge up the case again?"

"Because I'll never feel completely cleared of this matter until all the questions are answered. The sheriff and I had a talk yesterday. He told me that there are plenty of people who still think I had something to do with the express office robbery."

"Who cares what anyone else thinks? We're your friends. We know that you didn't have anything to do with it."

"There's more to it than that, Mary. Tom Elsworth was my friend too. I want to find the man who killed him."

Mary hung her head.

Steve gave an understanding look. "He's right, sis. As long as this robbery stays unsolved, Will will have a cloud over his head."

"Yes, I suppose so. But, Will, Charley was killed over a month ago. That's a cold trail. What do you hope to find that the sheriff didn't already uncover?"

"I don't know . . . maybe nothing . . . but it can't hurt to look."

"It's a far ride to Ridley, especially the way the roads are now," Mary put in.

"Yeah, I'll probably end up staying the night." He took another bite of a biscuit. "I don't remember much about Charley Ferris, but the two of you lived here in Coltonville some time before I arrived. Do you know anything about him?"

"Not much," Steve returned. "Charley was a loner. He got by on odd jobs and such. There were occasions when he would disappear for weeks at a time. When the story about him broke, Mary and I were surprised to hear that he was involved in such a thing."

Grant nodded. "That's the point. If you don't believe Charley's story, most other folks probably don't either."

Steve and Mary glanced at one another.

Finally, Steve stood up. "Well, we'd best be going. It was great seeing you again, Will." He shook Grant's hand. Turning to Mary, he said, "I'll wait for you in the wagon."

Grant helped Mary put on her wrap.

After Mary put on her hat, she placed her hands on Grant's arms. "I wrote to you while you were in prison. You wrote back . . . for a while. What made you stop?"

Grant took a deep breath and slowly released it. "After a time, I figured I'd be behind bars for the rest of my life. I couldn't see you wasting your time thinking about me. It wasn't fair to you."

"I thought it was something like that," she said as she smiled at him, relief in her voice. Squeezing his arms, she added, "Take care, Will. Let me know if you learn anything about Charley."

He walked out with her and helped her board the wagon.

"How about coming for dinner next Sunday?" Mary asked.

"Sounds good. I'll be there."

Mary waved as Steve picked up the reins and started the horses.

As Grant returned to his coffee and biscuits, he considered Mary and Steve. They were good people. They had supported him throughout his trial and had encouraged him with letters after he had been sent to prison. He knew that he could count on them now as he had before if he needed help. After he finished breakfast, he took down his Winchester from his gun rack. He located his backup .45 and holster rolled up in a drawer in his bureau. He cleaned and loaded both guns. He then strapped on the holster. At first it felt awkward, but as he moved, the weight of the .45 became less noticeable. He removed his heavy wool coat from the closet, brushed it off, and put it on. He picked up his gloves from a shelf and headed for the door.

Chapter Four

Herb Morton was seated in his small office at the bank when Grant was admitted by one of the tellers. He was a short man, barely five-feet-three, with thinning hair, a pencil mustache, and a silver pince-nez. He shook Grant's hand and waved him to a chair. Immediately, he instructed the teller to bring in Grant's file.

"Welcome, Will," he announced, smiling slightly. "It must feel good to be cleared after the ordeal you went through."

Grant nodded. "I have to start over again, Herb."

"Of course, and that's why we're here."

The teller brought in a folder, which he placed on Morton's desk. The bank president opened it and perused it quickly. "Well, your property taxes are all paid up, and

35

you have a balance of two-thousand-one-hundred-forty dollars and twelve cents."

"That's about what I figured."

"Are you planning on remaining in Coltonville, or are you considering selling your spread . . . because if you are, I can assure you, the bank will give you top price for your land."

Grant eyed Morton narrowly. He wondered if the banker might be making a subtle suggestion that it would be wiser for him to settle elsewhere. Morton had been accommodating enough following Grant's trial, when he agreed to handle Grant's finances. At the time, Grant looked upon it as an act of kindness from one neighbor to another, but perhaps it had been nothing more than a straightforward business arrangement, with an opportunity for the bank to continue to control his funds. He never trusted bankers, and he was not certain about Morton now. Maybe he should have allowed Ed Marley, his lawyer, to handle his finances. Marley had given him his money's worth at the trial, and his fee had been very reasonable. The two of them had had contract dealings before with the ranch, and Marley had proven to be a trustworthy man. Grant shrugged, for it was all water under the bridge now. Besides, he could be mistaken about Morton. "I don't know yet, Herb. I was tinkering with the idea of starting my herd again."

"Well, you're certainly solvent, and if you need additional funds, you can always take out a loan on your

spread. As far as the bank is concerned, you're good
for it."

"I just wanted to check. For now, I'll settle for some
money for supplies and out-of-pocket expenses."

"How much?"

"Let's say two hundred dollars."

Morton scribbled the amount on a piece of paper and
initialed it. "Hand this to the teller on your way out. He'll
take care of you."

They shook hands, Grant got his money, and left. As he
stood outside on the boardwalk, he could not help but recall Morton's words . . . *As far as the bank is concerned,
you're good for it.* It seemed like such a cold assessment
of a man. It had become a world of decimal points and
dollar signs. Whatever happened to a man's word or the
value of his efforts? Grant shook his head in disgust. At
least he had confirmed his recollection concerning his finances, and he did get a verbal guarantee for additional
funds if he needed them. Should anything go wrong,
should he fail in any way, the bank would certainly not be
the loser. As long as a man had collateral, the bank would
deal with him. There was nothing personal in it. Grant
stepped off the boardwalk and crossed the street, heading
toward Marley's office. The streets were as nearly deserted today as they had been yesterday when he arrived
on the train. It was still plenty cold. He could not blame
folks for sticking close to their fireplaces and stoves.

Marley had an office a block off the main street of
Coltonville. He had been one of the town's leading

attorneys for over five years. He had a solid reputation for his honesty and integrity. Marley shared an old clapboard building with a dressmaker. Grant passed by the window of Madame Elaine's and paused briefly to assess the latest fashions all the way from St. Louis. A mannequin displayed one of the fanciest dresses he had ever seen. He thought it strange that he had never seen any woman in Coltonville wearing such an outfit. He wondered about the practicality of such things as he moved past the window and entered Marley's outer office. The room was small but tidy. A few chairs, a potted plant, and some paintings of mountain scenes set the tone. Behind a desk off in one corner of the room sat Marley's secretary. Miss Raines was about sixty, frail looking, with a narrow nose and large doe eyes. Her gray hair was set in a neat bun. She wore a spotless gray blouse with tiny white buttons. A cameo brooch was the only jewelry she wore. When she saw Grant enter, she smiled warmly and rose to greet him.

"Oh, Mr. Grant, it's so good to have you back." She walked over and hugged him.

Grant smiled at her. "Thanks, Miss Raines. It's nice to see you again."

"You don't know how much Mr. Marley has grieved over your case. He's so relieved that it's at least partially resolved and you're free again."

"So am I."

"I'll tell him that you're here. He'll be delighted to see you."

"Thank you."

In a moment, she was ushering Grant into Marley's office. The lawyer greeted him at the doorway and wrung his hand vigorously. "Welcome home, Will!"

"It's good to be back, sir."

Marley led him to one of a pair of leather armchairs positioned in front of his long, highly burnished desk. On the desk were a blotter, some legal looking documents, several pens, an ink bottle, and a bronze statue of a mounted horseman. A lamp with a green shade cast a soft glow over the desk top. Behind the desk were shelves from ceiling to floor lined with law books.

"I appreciate that you kept me informed about Charley Ferris."

Marley settled into the high-backed chair behind his desk. He was about fifty, plump, and clean shaven, with a round face and bright friendly eyes. He was the kind of man who looked as if he were always in high spirits. "I wish I could have learned more, but the well seems to have gone dry. Charley was one of those people who just blended in with the wallpaper. As far as I've been able to ascertain, he left town a month or so after you were sent to prison. He was seen once or twice since then, but he didn't stick around. It appears that he took up residence over in Ridley. I sent a letter of inquiry to the sheriff there. He answered as many of my questions as he could, but he didn't really know much more about Charley either. Charley worked as a swamper and did a few other odd jobs—the same as he did here. He stayed in a room behind the saloon. As far as the sheriff could determine, there wasn't anyone in particular who had any significant contact with him."

"What about the shooting?"

"It was late. A gunshot was heard. They found Charley in his room, slumped over his bed. No one was seen in the area, and no one was heard riding away, but then Charley's room opened onto a back alley. Whoever shot him would have had an easy enough time escaping before the sheriff arrived on the scene. Charley was barely alive when they found him. He hung on for nearly an hour before he expired. Luckily for you, he survived long enough to clear you with his confession."

"And he named no one else?"

"If he had, there would have been a further investigation."

"The sheriff found no motive for the shooting?"

Marley shrugged. "That's the puzzling part. Charley had no known enemies. He wasn't robbed. He had only a few dollars in his possession, and the money was still in his pocket when they found him."

Grant's lips tightened.

Sensing his frustration, Marley said, "I know how you feel. No one wants to be left hanging on the end of a limb the way you are, but at least the case has come this far. We have to be thankful that you're free again."

"Somehow, I don't feel that that's enough."

Marley regarded him for a long moment. He then

picked up a pen, scribbled something on a piece of paper, and handed it to Grant.

Grant read the word TROWBRIDGE. Looking up at Marley, he saw the attorney leaning forward, eyeing him closely.

"The name of the sheriff in Ridley. You are going there, aren't you?"

"I am. How did you know?"

"I consider myself an excellent judge of character. It comes with my profession. I got to know you pretty well during the trial. I know how you think. I always believed that you were innocent. This reaffirms my opinion. A guilty man would never pursue this matter any further."

Grant smiled. "Thanks, Mr. Marley."

"I'll wire the sheriff, telling him to expect you. I'm sure he'll give you every cooperation, but I can't imagine that you'll discover anything new."

"Maybe not, but a different set of eyes can't hurt."

"Keep me posted."

"I will."

On his way out of town, Grant bought a large sack of oats. He wanted the bay to have a healthy portion before he started out for Ridley. He returned to his ranch house, where he separated the money he just withdrew from his account, leaving most of the bills in a bureau drawer of his china cabinet. He decided to take $50 with him to cover meals, lodging, and any emergency he might encounter. Next, he filled a canteen and made up a bedroll, which he secured to the horse.

It was just after eleven o'clock when he found himself on the road. He estimated the mercury well below freezing and dropping steadily. He could see air from the horse's nostrils rising upward. The sky was relatively clear, but a heavy cloud bank was moving in from the west. It would, most likely, add new snow to the layer that already covered the ground. The road was already deep in snow, and there were no signs of travelers. Grant moved the bay steadily but not fast. There was no reason to risk a mishap by pushing him too quickly. Half an hour more or less would make little difference to Grant. A year in prison had taught him patience. He had learned how to make time his ally.

His trip proved uneventful. He encountered only one other traveler on the road, a freighter on his way to Coltonville. They exchanged a few words about the weather and the road and then went their separate ways. It was simply too cold to linger.

By the time he brought the town of Ridley in sight, Grant was thoroughly uncomfortable. The temperature had plummeted and the wind had picked up. His ears were cold, his eyes were watering, and he felt as stiff as saddle leather. Riding down the main street, he spotted the sheriff's office immediately. He pulled up in front of it and dismounted. He tied the bay to a hitching rail and stepped onto the boardwalk. Glancing up and down the street, he saw only one person, heavily bundled up, trudging through the snow. Otherwise, the street was deserted. The only sound he heard was the sign over the gunsmith's shop two doors down, squeaking on its chains as it blew in the wind. Shivering, he entered the sheriff's office and quickly closed the door behind him.

The office was warm and inviting. He saw a short, stumpy man of about seventy placing chunks of wood into a stove. "Howdy, stranger," the man said in a friendly voice.

"Howdy," Grant returned as he glanced about the room. It was long but narrow. A desk, a few wooden chairs, and a side table were the only items of furniture. There were dodgers posted about the room as well as a map, yellow with age, tacked on one wall.

"Can I help you?"

The man's face was covered with a full beard. He had thick eyebrows and a bulbous nose.

"Is the sheriff about?"

"No, sir. He's on an errand, but he should be back shortly."

Grant nodded. He unbuttoned his coat and stepped over to the stove, where he removed his gloves and warmed his hands.

"Mite cold out, is it?"

"That it is."

The old-timer shook his head. "Think I'll just stay near the office today."

"Sounds like a good idea."

The man eyed Grant closely. "Don't believe I've seen you around here before, mister."

"I'm from Coltonville."

"Coltonville? That's a long ride to make on a day like this!"

"Too long to return today. It looks like it's going to snow again."

"That it will. I can feel it in these old bones."

"Is there a decent hotel in town?"

"Sure is. Two blocks south, across the street—the Hamilton House. Clean sheets, soft mattresses."

"I think I'll hole up there for the night."

"You won't regret it. How about some coffee? Warm your innards."

"I'd appreciate it."

The man grinned broadly. He hefted a charred pot and filled a cup, which he handed to Grant.

Grant took a sip as the steam escaped around his face. It went down well and warmed his stomach. The cup felt good in his fingers as well, which he could barely feel.

"How is it?" the man asked, squinting at Grant with an almost worried expression.

"It's probably the best coffee I've had in years."

The old-timer beamed proudly. "Sheriff Trowbridge tells me it's too strong, but I like it that way. Looks like you do too."

"I do, sure enough."

"Well, set yourself down and rest a spell."

Grant drew up a chair and sat down. Between the

coffee and the heat generated by the stove, he began to feel better again in about ten minutes.

A short time later the door opened, and with it came a rush of wind. A man bundled up in a heavy wool coat secured the door behind him, turned, and shrugged. "I swear . . . it seems to get colder every year." He glanced at Grant and then at the old-timer. Awkwardly, he stripped off his coat and hung it, along with his Stetson, on some hooks. Removing his gloves, he strode over to the stove and warmed his hands. He was about fifty-five, short, and stocky. His hair was thin, his face clean shaven except for a thick mustache. He regarded Grant for a long moment before he said, "You'd be Will Grant from Coltonville."

"That's right."

"I'm Sheriff Trowbridge. I got a wire today telling me that you'd be comin'. It must be important for a man to travel on a day like this."

Grant nodded.

"Ed Marley asked me to tell you all I know about Charley Ferris. Well, that won't take long." He glanced up at the old-timer. "Ben, would you fetch that box in the back room with Charley's effects."

"Yes, sir," the old man said before disappearing through a door. In a moment he was back toting a small wooden box, which he placed on Trowbridge's desk.

Trowbridge stepped up to the box, removed the contents, and waved Grant over. "These are Charley's belongings—everything he owned."

Grant sifted through each item. There were two faded

shirts, a worn pair of pants, a set of long johns, a bandanna, and a battered Stetson. All the pockets were empty. A small envelope contained two one-dollar bills, some coins, and a jackknife.

"This is it?"

"That's it. Not much of a legacy for a man to leave, is it?"

Grant shook his head. "Did Charley have any next of kin?"

"None that I've been able to find. There was a rumor that he had a daughter back East, but no one seems to know for sure."

Disappointed, Grant said, "I'd like to see his room."

"All right, but there's not much to see." Trowbridge pulled on his coat again, put on his Stetson, and led Grant across the street to the saloon.

The Red Garter was dimly lit inside. There were a few men in coats idling at the bar. A man wearing a black hat with a silver band and black clothes was sitting alone at one of the tables, a bottle and a deck of cards in front of him. They all glanced up when Trowbridge and Grant entered. Those at the bar nodded at Trowbridge and eyed Grant curiously. The man at the table did not pay much attention, as he seemed to be concentrating on his cards.

The bartender, a thin man with his hair slicked back, approached Trowbridge and greeted him.

"Sam, I'm goin' to take another look at Charley Ferris' room."

"Help yourself, Sheriff. It's not locked."

Trowbridge led Grant through a door and turned down a dark narrow hallway. He passed a few doors until he paused before the last room on the left of the passage. He opened the door, lit a lamp, and stood with his back to the wall.

Grant entered and looked around. A small bed, a bureau with a pitcher and basin, and a footstool were the only furnishings. A cracked mirror hung on one wall. Grant glanced around and then focused on Trowbridge.

"This is it, Mr. Grant. We found him right there on the bed. You can still see the bloodstains on the mattress. I figure whoever killed him must've left by the door at the end of the hallway and slipped out through the alley."

Grant opened the bureau drawers. He found nothing but a straight razor and a cake of soap. Under the bed, he pulled out a box that contained some half a dozen empty whiskey bottles. He looked up at Trowbridge, who raised his eyebrows. Grant stood silently in the middle of the room with his hands in his coat pockets and surveyed the scene. Again, he was disappointed. A box full of rags and a shabby corner room in the back of a saloon . . . it was all just a waste of time.

"Sorry there isn't anything more," Trowbridge put in.

"When I was in prison, my attorney mailed me a complete report of everything Charley said before he died. It was enough to clear me, but I need to know more. There's someone else involved in this. Is there anything else that you might have remembered since then . . . anything at all that could give me a lead?"

"No, nothing. Charley was clear at first, then he started to fade out. He mumbled some, but we couldn't make much of it."

Grant frowned. "Why would a man like this be murdered?"

Trowbridge shrugged. "This isn't Tombstone and I'm not Wyatt Earp. We don't have much crime here in Ridley. I've been the law here for ten years, and I generally don't have much more to do than lock up drunks or settle down unruly cowhands on a Saturday night. Charley wasn't robbed. I can't imagine him bein' in a fight. I'm just as puzzled by this as anybody."

"Yeah." Grant adjusted his Stetson and turned for the door.

"There is one thing . . ."

Grant eyed him closely.

"Charley was shot with a derringer."

"A derringer?"

"That's right. Doc Bradley removed a .22 rimfire cartridge from his heart."

"You know anybody around here who carries a derringer?"

"No. You see an occasional gambler sporting one, but most men carry side arms that pack more punch."

Grant nodded.

"I know you're disappointed, son, but there's only so much you can squeeze out of a rock. Why don't you come back to the office and we'll talk a spell."

Grant forced a smile. He followed Trowbridge out of

the saloon, and they made their way back to the sheriff's office.

Trowbridge shed his Stetson and his coat again and then eased into the chair behind his desk.

Grant unbuttoned his coat and sat in front of him.

Trowbridge shuffled through some papers and then leaned forward, resting his elbows on the desk. "You've been theorizin' that somebody else connected with your express office robbery had something to do with Charley's murder."

"I was hoping there was a connection."

"That doesn't seem likely, considerin' that the robbery took place a year ago."

Grant conceded the point.

"Yet it makes even less sense that someone from around here or even a stranger, for that matter, would be inclined to do away with Charley. There just wasn't any practical reason."

"None of it seems to make sense."

"I understand that the money from that holdup has never surfaced."

"That's what I heard."

"It's kind of crazy . . . Charley livin' the way he did . . . a couple of dollars in his pocket . . . after he took part in such a heist," Trowbridge mused.

"Yeah. It makes you wonder."

"It's a lot of money for someone to be sitting on. That kind of thing just runs contrary to human nature."

"That it does."

Trowbridge shoved some papers aside and leaned back in his chair. "Well, sorry I couldn't do more for you. What's your next move?"

"I don't know that I have one." Grant ran his fingers over his eyes.

Trowbridge opened a drawer and removed a bottle and two glasses. "Maybe a shot of this will help."

"No, I don't think so."

"It relaxes the brain . . . helps you to forget your problems."

"What I need is a decent night's sleep." Glancing out the window at the already falling snow, he added, "It's too late to return to Coltonville. I think I'll spend the night here and head back in the morning."

"Good idea," Trowbridge returned. "The hotel has a fine dining room. Ask for the apple pie."

The two men shook hands, and Grant left the office. He had spotted the livery on the way into town. He left the bay there for the night and headed for the Hamilton House. He signed the register and paid the desk clerk. His room was on the second floor. It was small but comfortable—and clean—as the old-timer at the sheriff's office had testified. The room's only window overlooked the main street. Grant watched the snow fall for a few minutes before he cleaned up and went down to the hotel dining room. He found that he had it all to himself. An old waiter brought him a limited menu and a steaming cup of coffee. Grant ordered a steak and fried potatoes and, taking the sheriff's advice, had a large slab of apple pie with a slice of cheese on it. The food was satisfying and tasty.

Before returning to his room, Grant picked up a three-day-old newspaper in the lobby. He sat in an armchair and read through it completely in fifteen minutes. Articles about the construction of a new school, the mayor's comments about the election of a Republican governor, and the fall in cattle prices were the main fare. He dropped the paper on the chair and climbed the stairs to his room. In a few minutes, he was in bed. For a while, he folded his hands behind his head and stared at the ceiling. Assessing the facts he had learned today, he concluded that he had ridden a long way for little, if anything. He did not know why Charley Ferris had died. He had failed to establish any connection between Charley's murder and the express office robbery. The two incidents might have been totally unrelated. The only point of interest that he discovered was that Charley had been shot with a derringer. That, in itself, was unusual but not necessarily significant. He had the impression that Trowbridge believed in his innocence and had genuinely tried to help him. Nevertheless, as the lawman had pointed out, there was only so much you could squeeze out of a rock. Grant sifted the facts over and over in his mind until his eyelids grew heavy. The last thing he remembered before falling asleep was the sound of the wind howling as thick flakes of snow struck against the window pane.

Chapter Five

Grant awoke early the next morning. A glance out the window told him that the snow had abated. In fact, the sky was clear, and the sun was peaking over the mountains in the distance. He washed and dressed and made his way to the dining room, which had considerably more patrons than it did on the previous evening. He enjoyed half a dozen buckwheat cakes, some bacon, and three cups of coffee. He then returned to his room to secure his belongings and headed for the livery to fetch the bay.

The ride back to his ranch was uneventful. He thought about Charley Ferris all the way. He could not conceive in any way how such a man could have been involved in the robbery of the express office. The simple truth of the matter was that it did not make sense. It was no wonder that there were those who questioned his release from prison. Furthermore, what had become of the money? Forty thousand dollars was a considerable sum. A man could do wonders with it. Why had it not yet surfaced? Was it possible that those responsible were dead as Sheriff Logan had suggested? Perhaps they had had a falling out and had killed one another. Perhaps the money lay buried somewhere—never to be found again. Grant shrugged. If that were the case, he would never know the truth about what happened that night at the express office, and his name would never be completely cleared. Maybe it would be better to sell his land and move elsewhere where no one knew him. He could start over again in a different part of the country.

His thoughts were mixed as he brought his ranch house into view. He reined in the bay and scanned the layout of the land. He had loved this spread from the moment he had set eyes on it. It had water, good pasture, and a solid house and barn. He had expected to live his life here. He had even held onto his land while he was in prison, hoping that his name would be cleared and he could return again. His spirits were once again lifted upon his release. He hoped that with Ferris' admission of guilt he would be able to resolve all questions concerning his involvement in the express office robbery. Now, with Ferris' death came another dead end. There were just as many unanswered questions as before.

Grant took a deep breath and released it slowly. He shook his head and cursed himself in disgust. Suddenly,

he was ashamed of himself. He had never run from anything before and he had no intention of running now. He
had also forgotten one thing—Tom Elsworth. His friend's
life had been cut short on that fateful night, and he had
vowed long ago that he would find those responsible. He
was here, and here he would stay . . . until he had all the
answers . . . until Tom's death was avenged.

He urged the bay forward and made his way into the
barn. He unsaddled the horse, rubbed him down, and
then walked to the house. He hung his hat and coat and
then unbuckled his holster and draped it over the back of
a chair. He started a fire, for the ranch house was bitterly
cold. He removed the money from his pocket and placed
it in the drawer of the china cabinet with the money he
had left behind. Hastily counting it, he concluded that he
would have enough to last for the better part of a month.
Next, he fired up the stove and made a pot of coffee. He
made a meal out of the rest of Mary's biscuits. He found
a pencil and a sheet of paper and proceeded to draw a di-
agram of the express office, the street in front, and the alley to the side and behind it. For the next twenty minutes,
he stared at the paper, replaying the night of the robbery,
sifting through every detail that he could recall in an effort to explain the events that had unfolded. He had done
it a hundred times during the year he had been in prison,
and he concluded this day in the same way he had every
other time, by crumpling up the paper and tossing it
aside.

He strolled over to his book shelf, selected a green-backed edition of a Charles Dickens novel, one of his favorites, and spent the rest of the evening in his chair next to the fireplace thumbing through it.

The following morning, after breakfast, Grant decided to ride into town. He wanted to see Ed Marley about his talk with Trowbridge. He also decided that he needed a horse on a permanent basis. The bay had served him well. He wondered if he were for sale. Hopefully, he could get a good deal from Lud Barrow at the livery. Setting aside some money for foodstuffs, he took the remainder of his cash from the drawer.

Barrow was sitting in his small office having a cup of coffee when Grant entered. He eyed Grant uneasily and then slowly climbed to his feet.

"Morning, Mr. Barrow. I've decided to buy a horse. Would the bay be for sale?"

Barrow rubbed his hand across the hair on his chin. It was obvious that he was doing some calculating in his head. "I suppose I could let him go. Would you be needin' a saddle as well?"

"No. I'll return this one the next time I'm in town."

"I see." Barrow pursed his lips. "How's sixty dollars sound?"

"A little high."

"Well, he's a sturdy enough horse."

"That he is. There's no denying that, but sixty is still a little steep for me. Could you come down a little?"

Barrow frowned.

"How about fifty?" Grant suggested.

"Fifty-two and he's yours."

Grant reached into his pocket and paid Barrow.

"I'll write you out a receipt," the ostler said as he quickly pocketed the money.

Grant patted the bay, and the animal nuzzled his shoulder.

Upon stopping by Ed Marley's office, Grant found the attorney out. Miss Raines greeted him warmly and explained that Marley was having stomach problems again and could be found at the cafe.

Grant rode the bay over to the eatery. It was a small building with a lunch counter for four and some half a dozen tables covered with checked cloths. One man was eating at the counter, and an elderly couple were having pie and coffee at the table nearest the door. Marley was off in a corner by himself, bent over a bowl of soup. He grinned when he saw Grant enter and waved him over.

The waitress, a pretty girl of about seventeen, approached as Grant pulled up a chair. She offered him a menu but he declined to order anything.

"Hello, Mr. Marley. Your secretary told me I could find you here," he said as he removed his coat and draped it over the chair beside him.

Marley rubbed his stomach. "My ulcer is acting up again. Sometimes it does me good to take in some food. Clear broth seems to help."

"How does an ulcer feel?"

"Like a toothache in your belly."

Grant grimaced.

"How was your trip?"

"I'm not sure it was worth the ride." He proceeded to relate his conversation with Sheriff Trowbridge, and he described his examination of Charley Ferris' room and belongings.

Marley listened intently as he spooned in his soup. When Grant mentioned that Charley had been shot with a derringer, Marley raised an eyebrow. "I didn't know about the derringer. It could prove significant."

"It's unusual."

Marley shrugged. "Maybe not as unusual as you might think."

Grant shot a questioning glance at him.

"I have one myself. I carry it sometimes when I'm traveling. Businessmen often carry derringers for protection . . . so do women."

Marley's remarks only served to deflate Grant's hopes that much further. He thought that he had discovered a solid clue toward identifying Ferris' killer. Now, he concluded that he was no closer.

Marley sensed his disappointment. He patted Grant's hand. "Patience is the rule when one is building a case. You discovered something that I didn't know, and I've been on this for a month. Who knows what it may mean? It's certainly something that we cannot discount."

Grant assented.

The door to the cafe opened and two men sauntered in. One was six-two, two hundred pounds, bearded, with rumpled clothes. The other was similar in appearance but a bit heavier. Grant recognized them as the Tarver brothers—Karl and Jonas. He had never particularly cared for them and, for that reason, never had much to do with them. He considered them rough cast, loud, and un-ruly. They glanced in his direction when they entered, exchanged a look, and then sat down at the counter. A minute passed while they ordered coffee before the one named Karl spun around on his stool and said in a voice that filled the room, "It smells like convict in here."

Grant turned toward him but Marley whispered, "Just ignore them. They like to spout off, but they'll go away if you don't pay them any mind."

"That's fine with me. I'm not looking for trouble."

"I guess somebody didn't hear me. I said it smells like convict in here," Karl repeated.

The man sitting at the far side of the counter placed a coin next to his plate and left.

Jonas turned around on his stool and smiled at his brother. "Yeah, they oughtta do something about who they serve in here."

Grant folded his hands on the table in front of him.

The waitress stood behind the counter, an anxious expression on her face.

"I wouldn't be overly concerned, Jonas. It looks like he's about to leave."

The two brothers chuckled loudly.

"Why don't we leave, Will. You don't want to tangle with those two," Marley whispered.

Grant leaned back in his chair. "Finish your soup, Mr. Marley."

"But, Will—"

Grant turned to the waitress. "Miss, I think I'll have a cup of coffee."

Marley shook his head as he rubbed his stomach.

The Tarvers suddenly stopped chuckling. Karl got off his stool and stepped over to the table, where he stood next to Marley. "Lawyer, you'd best watch whose company you keep."

Marley looked up at Tarver. "Karl, Will Grant is a free man. He has the right to come and go as he pleases, and you have no business interfering with him. Why don't you just go back to the counter and finish your meal. Nobody's bothering you."

"That's where you're wrong. This ex-convict is troublin' me some."

Grant stared straight ahead while the waitress poured his coffee with a shaky hand.

"Did you hear me, Grant? I don't like the smell of you."

"How's your soup, Mr. Marley?" Grant asked calmly.

Karl's expression soured quickly. He placed his hand under Marley's bowl and flipped it over onto the floor.

The waitress gasped as she stepped away from the table and stood with her back to the wall.

The elderly couple stood up and moved toward the door.

Jonas was laughing aloud from his stool.

"Oh, I sure am sorry, Mr. Lawyer, but accidents do happen."

"Miss, bring Mr. Marley another bowl of soup," Grant instructed. "Mr. Tarver will pay for it."

Karl glared down at Grant with a twisted sneer. Placing his hand on Grant's shoulder, he began to dig his fingers into Grant's flesh. "Mister, I'm about to squash you like a bug."

Grant slowly raised his right hand and took hold of Karl's wrist. Despite the downward pressure that the man exerted, Grant managed to remove Karl's hand from his shoulder and force it farther and farther away an inch at a time. It was not the easiest thing that Grant had ever done, but then again, he did not exactly strain a muscle to accomplish it. Finally, Karl backed away and, rubbing his wrist, stared hard at Grant. Grant rose to his feet and squared off against the bigger man. Suddenly, Karl doubled up his fist and reared back, but before he had time to deliver a blow, Grant shot out his left, connecting solidly with Karl's nose, jarring him, forcing him to stagger backwards. For a moment, Karl stood there awkwardly, staring at Grant as a bead of blood trickled down his nose and onto his lips. Enraged, Karl's eyes widened and he lunged toward Grant. Grant easily sidestepped him and rammed his fist into Karl's ribs as he passed by. Karl recovered his balance, turned, kicked a chair out of his path, and came at Grant again. He swung wildly but did not even come close to making contact. Grant countered with a sharp jab with his left that connected with Karl's mouth and followed with a right that dropped the big man to the floor.

When Jonas saw his brother go down, he came off his stool and waded into Grant more cautiously. Grant held his ground, his fists raised in a defensive posture. Jonas feigned a left and then followed with a roundhouse right. Grant averted most of the force of the blow, but it did catch him on the shoulder. Off balance now and leaving himself open, Jonas tried to back away, but Grant seized his advantage. Dropping his right shoulder, he slammed his fist into Jonas' midsection. Jonas' breath escaped in a soft wheeze as he clutched his stomach in pain. Grant moved in and delivered an uppercut to Jonas' chin. It lifted Jonas off his feet and dropped him against the counter, where he struck his back hard before sliding down to the floor between two of the stools.

Grant then stepped back to the table and put on his coat.

Marley regarded him in stunned surprise.

The couple near the door sat down again, uncertain as to what they had just witnessed.

Karl was sitting up, rubbing his jaw as he shot a baleful look at Grant. "This doesn't change a thing. You may be walkin' the streets, but there are still plenty of people in this town who believe that you robbed that express office and got away with murder."

Grant picked up his cup and tossed the coffee into Karl's face.

Karl bellowed as the searing liquid struck him. He pressed his fingers to his eyes and cursed through gritted teeth.

As Grant and Marley stood on the boardwalk in front of the cafe, the lawyer said, "I'll speak to the sheriff about what happened here. If you want to press charges, I'm sure the other witnesses will cooperate."

"Forget it."

"All right, but if I know the Tarver brothers, they aren't through . . . and the next time, they may use more than their fists."

"I can take care of the Tarver brothers."

Marley nodded. "By the way, where did you learn to handle yourself like that?"

"My cell mate in prison was an ex-prizefighter. He taught me how to defend myself, and I helped him to write letters to his grandson."

Chapter Six

Grant was a quarter of a mile from his spread when he encountered another rider approaching in his direction. It was a woman astride a small paint. She wore a gray coat and a matching gray hat with a small red plume in it. She reined in her horse and turned in front of Grant, effectively blocking his path. Upon closer scrutiny, he saw that she was a most attractive woman with auburn hair, large brown eyes, and a fair complexion. "Mr. Grant?" she inquired.

"I'm Grant."

"My name is Nora Masters. I'm a reporter for *The Tribune*."

"Yes?"

"I came out to ask you for an interview for my paper."

"No, I—"

"Your story is unusual, and I thought my readers would be interested in hearing about the year you spent in prison, your feelings about your release, and your thoughts about the payroll—which is still missing."

"I'm not interested, Miss Masters." Grant turned the bay in an effort to pass her, but Nora reached toward him and checked his reins.

"There is something that might interest you."

He regarded her angrily.

"There's a man out at your place."

"Who is he?"

"I don't know. I never saw him before. I thought it might be you, but then I realized it wasn't. I saw you only once before—in town—but I knew it wasn't you. He put his horse in your barn and went into your house."

Grant considered her words carefully. "Thanks. You'd best ride back into town now."

"Do you want me to notify the sheriff?"

"No. I'll handle it myself."

"Whatever you say." She placed her hand on his arm. "Be careful."

Grant felt there was a genuine sincerity in her tone and a look of concern in her eyes. He nodded and rode onward. Not wishing to alert his uninvited visitor, he diverted from the road and approached the barn from the rear, so as not to be seen from the house. He tied the reins of the bay to a post near the back door of his barn. He opened the door slowly and peeked inside. As Nora Masters had indicated, there was a horse in the first stall—a big sorrel, still saddled. A Winchester rested in the scabbard. Grant did not recognize the brand. He made his way around the barn, advancing toward his house from the rear. When he reached his bedroom, he opened the window carefully, to avoid any sound. Cautiously, he parted the curtains and slipped in. His bedroom door was slightly ajar, and he could hear noises coming from the kitchen. He drew his .45 and entered the hallway. He saw nothing, but he detected the aroma of coffee. Puzzled, he inched his way down the hallway and peered around the corner. He was surprised to see a man dressed in a dark suit sitting at his table drinking coffee. Grant watched him for a full minute before confronting him. Cocking his .45, he aimed it squarely at the man's chest. The man heard the click of the hammer and turned suddenly, spilling some of the coffee on the table.

"Don't shoot. I mean you no harm."

Grant walked up to him, his gun still trained on his chest.

"I'm not armed," the man announced, placing the cup on the table, standing slowly, and raising his hands.

He was about forty, five-eight, one hundred sixty pounds. He had a square jaw and a thin mustache. He wore no holster. "My name's Dunbar . . . Frank Dunbar."

"Don't move a muscle," Grant ordered as he reached toward the man with his free hand and patted him down. In Dunbar's inside coat pocket, Grant felt something hard. He removed a silver flask, which he set on the table. In the opposite side pocket, Grant discovered a small revolver, which he lifted carefully and slipped into his own coat pocket.

Dunbar looked at him sheepishly. "I forgot about that. You see, I've never had any call to use it. Most of the time, I don't even remember that it's there."

"Now, Mr. Dunbar, suppose you tell me who you are and what it is that you're doing in my house."

"Sure . . . sure, but do you mind?" he said, lowering his hands slowly.

Grant nodded.

"I made myself some coffee. I hope you don't mind. You see, I didn't have anything to eat yet today."

"Sit down, but keep your hands where I can see them."

"Of course." Dunbar sat down and picked up the cup.

Grant sat down opposite Dunbar, his gun still trained on him.

"I'm a businessman. I came out here to make you a proposition."

"What kind of proposition?"

"I know your story. I know all about you—I mean the express office robbery, the time you spent in prison . . . everything."

Grant said nothing but eyed him closely.

"I know that the money has never turned up, and—"

"And you thought that I was sitting on it."

Dunbar grinned. "Let's just say that I thought it was a strong possibility."

"There seem to be several others who share your opinion."

"As I said, it is a possibility—certainly one worth exploring."

"Go on."

Dunbar took a sip of coffee. "I'm what you might call an investor. I invest other people's money, and I double it. I don't ask where they got it or how they came by it."

"And you're looking for a little capital to invest?"

"That's the idea. Now, if you happen to have that money, the chances of you spending it within five hundred miles of here are practically nonexistent. The law's watching, and so are others. On the other hand, I'm not from these parts. I have connections with a syndicate back East. I handle large sums of money all the time. I could serve as an outlet . . . invest some or all of that payroll, and in . . . oh, say . . . two years . . . maybe less . . . I can double it for you. Your hands wouldn't touch it. People could watch you all they want but you'd be clean. When your investment matures, I could arrange to have your money safely deposited in a bank back East—minus a small cut for my services, of course. After an additional two years, things will have cooled down and . . . well, you get the picture."

Grant listened with interest to Dunbar's proposal. When Dunbar concluded, Grant regarded him for a long moment. "Well, Mr. Dunbar, suppose I were to tell you that I was never involved in that robbery and that I know nothing about the money?"

Dunbar leaned back in his chair and smirked. "Come now, Mr. Grant. We're both . . . men of experience."

Grant smiled. He rose to his feet and holstered his weapon.

Dunbar gave him a satisfied glance as he raised the cup to his lips.

Grant leaned across the table and backhanded Dunbar across the face, knocking the cup from his hand and shattering it against the wall.

Dunbar's eyes widened as he stared at Grant in shock, coffee dribbling down his chin.

"Don't bother about cleaning up the mess. I'll take care of it myself," Grant said coolly.

Dunbar removed a handkerchief from his pocket and proceeded to dab his face and his suit.

"Now, get your horse out of my barn and be off my property in five minutes."

Dunbar stood up quickly and turned for the door.

Grant stood in front of the window and watched Dunbar enter the barn. In less than a minute, he emerged on horseback. Dunbar shot a glance over his shoulder toward the house before riding off. Grant waited until he disappeared from view. He removed Dunbar's handgun from his coat pocket and examined it. It was light—barely more than a pound. He had seen weapons like it before. It was a Webley Bulldog—small and easily concealed. He placed it on his mantlepiece and shook his head in disgust. "Now they're even invading my home."

Nora Masters was not surprised by Will Grant's refusal to talk with her. She sensed that he had become withdrawn, even guarded about his past. It was something she had suspected even before she decided to approach him. Nevertheless, she thought her overture might be worth a try. For her article on the express office robbery, she had been trying to interview as many townsmen who had served on Will Grant's jury as possible. She discovered, however, that many of the locals had been as difficult to interview as was Grant. The first juror she approached did not want to be questioned. The second slammed his door in Nora's face. The next two were courteous enough but could offer nothing above and beyond the old articles published by *The Tribune*. On her next try, she was pleasantly surprised to learn that Vin Ericson, the foreman of the jury, would be willing to contribute to her article. In fact, he even invited her to his ranch for lunch.

Ericson was a prosperous rancher. He had a large spread east of town. Nora rode out, eager to meet with someone who might be able to shed some additional light on the mystery that shrouded Will Grant and the town of Coltonville. Despite her heavy coat, she found herself half frozen by the time she reached Ericson's ranch house. It was a rambling structure, two stories, four gables, white in color with a brown roof. It was nothing fancy; it looked like the serviceable residence of a working rancher. There were many corrals and out-buildings, along with the largest barn Nora had seen since she reached Montana. Ericson, himself, stepped out on the porch to greet her. He was a big man—six-six, two hundred seventy pounds. He wore a beige flannel shirt and a brown corduroy coat. He had a thick crop of wavy chestnut hair and a coarse mustache that was one shade darker. A genuine smile rounded out a face that was a bit on the fat side but was, at the same time, warm and pleasant. He took Nora's arm and escorted her inside, where he took her coat and hung it on a peg. He then led her into a long comfortable-looking room fitted with a massive settee and half a dozen stuffed armchairs. A stone fireplace ran from floor to ceiling on the far side of the room. Several large logs reposed between a pair of andirons from which a blazing fire crackled, generating enough heat to soothe the farthest corners of the room.

"Sit down by the fire, Miss Masters, and take the chill out of your bones."

"Thank you. I am very cold," Nora replied as she slipped into a deep cushioned chair beside the hearth.

"These Montana winters are enough to chill even a hardy Viking like me," he announced with an enormous laugh. He sat down opposite her and folded his hands across his massive stomach.

Nora removed her gloves and took her pencil and note paper from her purse. "I'd like to thank you for agreeing to see me, Mr. Ericson."

"It's my pleasure."

"As you know, Will Grant's conviction was overturned last month, and he's returned to Coltonville."

"So I've heard."

"I was recently hired by *The Tribune,* and I'm re-searching an article about the express office robbery and the trial of a year ago. Since I'm not from these parts, I pretty much have to start from scratch. I've read all the old articles published in *The Tribune,* of course, and I've become fascinated with the case. I thought it might be in-teresting for the readers if I were to feature some follow-up thoughts of some of the citizens. In particular, I'd like to see if any members of the jury have changed their opinions about Mr. Grant, and I hoped that someone might come up with a different perspective as to who ac-tually committed the robbery and where the money might be."

"I see."

"I've been trying to interview some of those who served on the jury, but so far I've met with little success. Some have little to contribute, and others don't even want to talk to me."

Ericson chuckled. "Well, don't be too hard on 'em. It's just human nature. Now that Grant's been freed, it's only normal for those of us who sat in judgement to have second thoughts. Some probably even feel some shame."

"How do you feel?"

Ericson took a deep breath and let it out slowly. "I can walk with my head held high. Based on all the evidence,

I thought he was guilty. If I was faced with the same facts today, I'd vote the same way. As far as I'm concerned, there just wasn't any other choice."

"What was the most damning evidence against him?"

"That's easy. We all agreed on that. Grant claimed that somebody else had to be in the express office. His story was that somebody he didn't see shot Tom Elsworth and then shot him . . . yet there wasn't anybody else there. The sheriff and his deputy made a thorough search of the office. It was as simple as that. His story just didn't wash."

Nora jotted down Ericson's remarks. "Did you know Will Grant personally?"

"I knew who he was. In fact, I had a little deal goin' with him for the sale of one of my mares. He dropped by my spread . . . oh, I'd say a day or two prior to the robbery. The truth of the matter is that he was mighty interested in a couple of my horses. He couldn't seem to decide what he wanted. I had a set price in mind but he hadn't agreed to it. I got the impression that he didn't have the money." Ericson hesitated. "No, that's not fair. I should say that I got the impression that he didn't want to meet my price. We haggled a little, but before any sale could be made he was arrested."

Nora continued to scribble notes to herself. "What about Charley Ferris?"

"Charley was the kind of man you could pass on the street and not even notice. As far as I know, he had only one enemy—whiskey."

"Could he have truly been the kind of man who was involved in the robbery?"

"Miss Masters, that's a mighty hard question to answer. I would've said no, but then I recall a gal I met in my younger days when I was passin' through San Francisco. She was the prettiest, daintiest thing I'd ever seen. She turned out to be one of the city's leading pickpockets."

Nora smiled. "I get your point." She folded her papers and placed them in her purse. "Off the record, how do you think Will Grant will be accepted around Coltonville?"

Ericson passed his hand across his jaw. "If Grant is truly innocent, I'm glad he's a free man again. On the other hand, if he's guilty . . . well, then I believe there's been a miscarriage of justice. I'll do my best to keep an open mind. I imagine most folks around here will try to do the same."

Nora nodded. She thought Ericson was straightforward and honest. He was the kind of man she believed she could respect.

Nora agreed to stay on for lunch. They sat at a long pine table in a spacious dining room, where they were served by an old Indian woman who shuffled about in moccasins. Like everything else about Vin Ericson, the portions of food offered in his house were big. They lunched on roast beef sandwiches, mashed potatoes, and mugs of steaming hot coffee. Nora left the table full and content and well reinforced for the ride back to town.

As she rode back to Coltonville, she mulled over everything Ericson had told her. One thing was certain. Ferris' confession may have freed Grant, but it did not shed any light on the actual facts surrounding his case. The robbery was still a mystery and, perhaps, would remain so forever. Her concentration was broken when she happened to glance at the road behind her as she was negotiating a sharp turn. A blur of bright red caught her eye. She looked more closely and thought she detected a lone rider far in the distance. When she reined in her horse and turned, he vanished. Ten minutes later, she thought she saw him again, but once more he disappeared from view. She slipped her hand into her coat pocket and felt her derringer there. It reassured her somewhat but she still felt uncomfortable. She peered over her shoulder several more times as she continued toward town, but she did not see the rider again. Whoever it was was not keeping to the road. She dismissed him in time as one of Ericson's hands or simply as a stranger crossing the prairie.

Chapter Seven

Late the following morning Grant was stoking his fire when he heard a horse approaching. He stepped to the window and saw a young man riding a chestnut. He was not more than twenty-two, wore a white Stetson and a thick brown coat. A handgun was holstered on the outside of the coat. Grant watched him dismount and drop his reins over the hitching rail. As he stepped onto the porch, Grant spotted a badge on his coat. There was a knock on the door, and Grant opened it.

"Mr. Grant?" the man asked. He was clean shaven with pale blue eyes. Upon closer inspection, Grant concluded that he looked nearer eighteen.

"Yes."

"I'm Deputy Orr. Sheriff Logan sent me to fetch you."

"What's this all about?"

"I can't say, sir. I was just told to bring you in."

"Am I under arrest?"

Orr stood on the porch uneasily. "No, sir. The sheriff would just like a word with you."

"All right."

"Grant started to reach for his holster but the deputy said, "Would you leave your gun behind?"

Grant glanced at the youngster. Realizing that the deputy was just doing his job, Grant did not wish to create a problem for him. He left his .45 in its holster and took only his hat and coat.

Sheriff Logan was sitting behind his desk when Grant walked into his office. Nora Masters was standing beside him. She was wearing a beige dress with small pearl buttons that ran from a lace collar all the way down to her waist. Without her winter coat, she looked quite slender. She appeared altogether fresh and new, and she seemed somehow out of place standing in the sheriff's office amidst the array of rifles and faded wanted posters.

"Sit down, Will," Logan said.

Grant unbuttoned his coat and pulled up one of the wooden chairs in front of Logan's desk.

The deputy stood behind Grant, leaning against the wall.

"Do you know Miss Masters?"

"We've met," Grant replied, nodding to her.

"Hello again, Mr. Grant. I trust you were able to resolve the matter we discussed yesterday?"

"I was."

Logan glanced at the two of them and raised his eyebrow.

"What's this all about, Sheriff?"

Logan rested his arms on his desk. "Lud Barrow tells me that you bought a horse from him yesterday."

"That's right."

"That bay you've been riding?"

Grant nodded. "If Barrow claims I didn't pay for it, I still have the bill of sale."

"No, that's not the problem."

"Then what is it? What have you been doing anyway . . . following me around town checking up on me?"

"It's my job to check up on you, just as it's my job to recover the money stolen from the express office."

"The money from the express office? What are you talking about?"

Logan picked up an envelope and removed some currency. He placed it in front of him and eyed Grant closely. "Are these the bills you used to pay Barrow?"

Leaning forward, Grant saw three twenty-dollar bills. "I don't know for certain. If Barrow says they are, then I suppose they are. What about them?"

"Two of these twenty-dollar bills came from the express office robbery."

Grant was stunned. The words went through him like hot lead. For a time, he could not even speak. He leaned forward and picked up the bills, examining them closely. "That's impossible!"

"I'm afraid not. I have the list of serial numbers of the stolen notes right here, and two of these twenties match the numbers on it. There's no doubt about it."

Grant scanned the serial numbers in disbelief. "But I got that money from the bank. I withdrew it the day after I came back to town."

"Herb Morton confirmed that withdrawal, but both he and the teller claim that these notes did not come from the bank. You see, the bank also has this list of serial numbers."

Grant could not digest what Logan was telling him.

"Did you have any other money with you when you came to town? Something you got on the way?"

"No. I only had the money I was given when I left prison. It was a small amount . . . nothing close to a twenty. The only twenties I had I got from the bank." Grant continued to stare at the bills as though they were not there in his hands.

"You didn't get them in change . . . from some merchant in town, for instance?"

"No."

"You rode to Ridley. You stayed there overnight. Ridley was where Charley Ferris lived. Could you have picked up the bills there?"

Grant sensed that Logan was trying to give him a way out. "No. I'm certain that the only twenty-dollar bills I had came from the bank here in Coltonville."

Logan frowned as he took the money from Grant and

replaced it in the envelope. "In that case, it appears that we have a dilemma."

Grant racked his brain to recount the events of each day since his release from prison, but he could conceive of no reasonable explanation for having the bills in his possession. "I know how this looks, but do you think I would be foolish enough to rob the express office, hide the money, and then return to spend it . . . right here in Coltonville . . . within days after I got back?"

"He has a point, Sheriff. Only a fool would be so obvious," Nora observed.

"A fool . . . or a very cunning man," Logan returned.

"Now look, Sheriff, I've always claimed that I had nothing to do with the robbery of the express office. If I was truly trying to convince people of my innocence, do you think that—even if I had the money—I would spend it on a horse and stick around town just waiting for someone to find out about it?"

"I have to admit . . . it seems unlikely," Logan replied, rubbing his chin. "Do you have any other twenties?"

"No. I have no others."

"Nothing larger?"

"No." Grant removed the bills he carried in his pocket and placed them on Logan's desk. "There's more at home, but nothing as large as a twenty."

"All the money that came from the express office robbery was twenties and fifties."

"I have nothing left that's any larger than a ten."

"It appears as though someone is doing a good job of making Mr. Grant look guilty," Nora said. "Let's assume, for Mr. Grant's sake, that he is innocent. What better time could the real thief choose to implicate him than the week he was released from prison? Now that the money has surfaced again, the real thief is free and clear to start spending the money, and Mr. Grant will be suspect."

Logan smiled at Nora.

"If you put Mr. Grant in a cell, it's my guess that the money will dry up. On the other hand . . . if you allow him to walk free, the real thief may continue to spread the money, which will give you that much more of a chance of finding him."

"That makes good sense, Miss Masters. Besides, things seem to happen around Mr. Grant here."

"You're not going to hold me then?"

"Not for the time being. My deputy and I won't be far. I'll expect you to stay around Coltonville."

"I told you before, Sheriff, I'm planning to stay."

Grant and Nora Masters stood on the boardwalk in front of the sheriff's office, buttoning their coats. Grant looked at her admiringly. "That's the second time you came to my rescue, Miss Masters. I figure I owe you."

She smiled at him. "Does that mean that I get an interview after all?"

He returned her smile. "No."

She frowned.

"Would you settle for lunch instead?"

She smirked.

He liked the way the corners of her mouth curled up, and he liked the line of her cheekbones.

"I guess lunch would be better than nothing, but under the present circumstances . . . I think I'd feel more comfortable if I paid for it."

He chuckled. "All right. I'll be your guest this time." He took her arm, and they walked across the street to the hotel dining room.

Forty-five minutes later, they were finishing their dessert of apple pie and coffee. Their conversation had been light and pleasant. Despite the fact that she wanted information from Grant, Nora did not pressure him in any way. Instead, she allowed him to discuss those aspects of his life that he wished to share. He respected that in her, and because of it, he felt at ease with her. He told her about his boyhood in Ohio, about his years working on a ranch in Wyoming, and how he had inherited his spread in Coltonville from an uncle. Nora, in turn, spoke about her Missouri roots, her journey west, and her desire to work on a big city newspaper someday. She had come to Coltonville only a month ago in response to an advertisement she had seen about a position for a reporter. She had interviewed with Mr. Creighton, editor of *The Tribune,* and was hired. The conversation had been agreeable but it was inevitable that it should turn to the matter at hand.

"How do you think you actually came to have the money from the express office?"

"I've been considering that. I carry some of my money on me, but I leave some of it at home in a drawer of my china cabinet. It isn't exactly hidden. Anyone could have gotten into my house and found it. The stolen bills could have been exchanged for the twenties I got from the bank. I wouldn't have noticed the difference. The man, for instance, that you saw entering my house yesterday could have easily searched and found my money."

"When did you buy your horse?"

Grant frowned. "Yesterday morning . . . before I met you . . . and before I confronted the man at my ranch."

"Then, it couldn't have been him."

"That's true. It had to be someone else. My guess is that the switch probably took place the day I was in Ridley."

"Someone certainly did an excellent job of implicating you."

"Yeah, I have to admit . . . I must look like the prize scapegoat of all time."

She smiled. "Well, I must be going. I have a column to finish on the new millinery. Not exactly the kind of article I want to write, but a new reporter has to start somewhere."

He rose from his chair. "Thanks for the meal. Maybe the next time I can pay."

Grant watched Nora walk away. She had promised not to press him for an interview, and she kept her word. He respected her for that; however, there was one topic that had come up during their conversation that she did not pursue. That was the man she had seen at his ranch house. She had failed to ask anything about him or his reason for trespassing on Grant's property. Perhaps it had slipped her mind, as their conversation had changed directions so many times. Yet it was a matter that an inquiring reporter should have pursued. He wondered about Nora Masters and her intentions. Did she truly believe in his innocence, or was she simply angling for a story—a story that she might not be able to write if he were sitting in a jail cell? He spent the remainder of the day thinking about Nora Masters.

Nora climbed the stairs to the second floor of the hotel and located her room. She entered and locked the door behind her. As she hung her coat, she eyed the man sitting in a chair next to her bed. "I just had lunch with Will Grant," she announced.

Frank Dunbar nodded. "Well, congratulations. What's your impression?"

"He's intelligent . . . and interesting."

"He also won't be pushed," he returned, massaging his jaw.

"I talked the sheriff into keeping him out of jail for the time being, at least."

"That's good. It won't serve us if he's sitting behind bars. With Grant loose, we'll have a better chance of operating."

"Do you know that he even suggested the possibility that you might have been the one who switched the stolen bills with his."

"Really?"

"I helped to point out that he spent those bills before you visited his ranch."

"Hmm."

"What do we do next?"

"For now, we do nothing. Circumstances will dictate our next move."

Chapter Eight

Mary Collins set a nice dinner table. Fried chicken, mashed potatoes and gravy, greens, biscuits, and chocolate cake proved to be one of the best spreads Grant had enjoyed in a long time. Following the meal, he joined Mary and Steve in the parlor, where they sat in front of the fireplace and drank their coffee.

"Your house looks elegant. It seems larger than I remembered. What did you do while I've been gone?" Grant remarked.

"I enlarged the parlor and remodeled the kitchen. Mary's been complaining about how cramped everything was in the house ever since we bought it. I finally got around to doing something about it."

"Steve worked hard on it. The kitchen was so small I

could barely turn around without bumping my elbows. Now, I've room to spare."

"You've done well."

They went on to discuss the amount of snow they got during the winter, the slow arrival of spring, and cattle. In time, the topic came around to the express office robbery and the twenty-dollar bills that had just surfaced.

"The appearance of that money proves one thing," Steve announced. "The real thief is still in the area."

"It looks that way," Grant replied.

"The money was obviously used to implicate you, Will," Mary added.

"It certainly looks bad. I was a hairsbreadth away from a warm cell. As it is, every move I make will be watched."

"Why don't you just leave . . . start over again somewhere else?"

"Steve!" Mary objected.

"Well, you have to look at the facts, Mary. What kind of future does Will really have if he stays on in Coltonville? I hear that Oregon is a beautiful place to settle. I, for one, have always been interested in seeing California."

"Still talking about the coast, are you, Steve?" Grant asked with a smile.

"I'm tired of all this snow and cold. I've got Mary half-talked into leaving, but now that you're back, I'm not sure I can count on her," he said, winking at Grant.

Mary blushed.

"He's got a point, Mary."

"No man should be forced away from his ranch . . . his town . . . because of suspicions," Mary countered.

"Well, don't worry. I promised the sheriff I'd stick around. Actually, he more or less ordered me not to leave town, so even if I wanted to, I couldn't. Besides, I've decided to stay, and that's final."

Mary smiled at him. "Oh, I'm glad, Will."

Grant took a sip of his coffee and stared at the flickering flames. "What I can't figure is why that money never turned up before."

"That is strange," Steve returned. He placed his cup on the hearth and leaned forward in his chair. "Tell me, when you rode over to Ridley, did you learn anything about Charley Ferris?"

"Not really. Nobody seemed to know anything about him. A saloon swamper isn't exactly a newsworthy citizen."

"I'm glad his confession got you out of prison, but I have to admit . . . I still find it hard to believe that he could have had anything to do with that robbery. From what I remember, he never even carried a gun."

"I can't say I disagree with you. According to Sheriff Logan, there are others in town who share your opinion . . . the Tarver brothers, for instance."

"What about the Tarvers?"

Grant went on to relate his encounter with them in the cafe.

"Those brutes! Imagine people like them walking the

streets of Coltonville while Will's integrity is in question," Mary put in.

"The Tarvers are hardcases," Steve agreed. "You should have pressed charges against them."

Grant shrugged. "I don't think they'll be bothering me for a while. Besides, a stretch in jail might only sour their dispositions that much more."

"Well, no matter how things turn out, Will, you know you can always count on Mary and me."

"Thanks, Steve. It's good to have friends a man can rely on."

They talked for a while about their spreads and about Coltonville. Finally, Steve rose from his chair and said, "I'm for bed. I've got a big day ahead of me. I have to repair some of the church pews tomorrow morning, and then I have to work in the express office in the afternoon. I'll say good night." He shook Grant's hand and then retired, leaving Mary and Grant alone by the fire.

Mary moved closer to him and placed her hand on his arm. "Will, what Steve said is how it is. You know we'll always be here for you . . . no matter what."

Grant took her hand in his and smiled at her. Slowly, he pulled her toward him.

Later in the week, there was news of a stage holdup five miles outside of Ridley. Nora Masters wrote about it in her column in *The Tribune*. In her article, she reported that both the driver and the only passenger— a woman—were robbed and killed. According to the passenger manifest for the stage line, the woman's name was Adele Ferris. Nora went on to describe the scene of the shootings and to detail Sheriff Trowbridge's investigation, to date.

Grant read over the column twice and then decided to call on Nora. She was sitting at her desk in the office of *The Tribune* when Grant entered. She looked up from a litter of paperwork and smiled at him. "Hello, Mr. Grant, won't you be seated."

Grant pulled up a chair and sat down beside her, resting his arm on the edge of her desk. "I read your column."

"I thought it would be of interest to you. Details are a little sketchy, but I can tell you this. Sheriff Trowbridge of Ridley discovered that a woman resident of his town had been acquainted with Charley Ferris well enough to know that he had a daughter living in the St. Louis area. She wrote to the daughter, informing her of her father's passing. The daughter responded to the woman's letter, explaining that she would be traveling to Ridley to visit her father's grave and to call on her cousin, who also resided in the area."

"Then Adele is Charley's daughter."

"Yes. Unfortunately, we don't know the identity of Adele's cousin. There are no other residents in this area with the name Ferris. Therefore, Charley's cousin must have a different name. As luck would have it, Adele did not reveal it in her letter to Charley's woman friend in Ridley."

"You interviewed her?"

"Yes. I've been to Ridley. I met Sheriff Trowbridge and the woman in question. Her name is Esther Miles. She was able to provide us with an address for Adele Ferris. Sheriff Trowbridge sent a wire to St. Louis, asking the local law to make inquiries into Adele's background in the hopes of learning the identity of her cousin. He's going to keep me posted of any development."

"Well, that's something anyway."

"It's a chance."

"Ed Marley would be interested in hearing about this, but he's out of town on business." Grant drummed his fingers on the desk as he stared out the window. "I wonder . . . Adele Ferris may have written to her cousin as well, telling of her trip to Ridley."

Nora's eyes widened.

"Her letter would have gone through the post office at Ridley—the same as the letter she sent to Esther Miles, and—"

"And the postmaster might just remember the name Adele Ferris on the envelope," Nora put in, quickly picking up on Grant's idea. "I'll send a wire to Sheriff Trowbridge immediately."

Grant raised his finger. "Adele Ferris may not have put her name or her return address on the envelope of her letter. Many people don't. Even so, her letter would still have had the St. Louis postmark on it."

Nora nodded her understanding. "I'll ask Sheriff Trowbridge to inquire about every letter bearing the

St. Louis postmark received in Ridley starting . . . a week after Charley's death."

"Thanks. I'd appreciate it if you'd let me know as soon as you hear anything."

"I will."

The reply to Masters' telegram arrived late the next day but it bore no fruit. The Ridley postmaster had received no other letters from Adele Ferris. Only two other letters, in fact, had arrived bearing the St. Louis postmark. One was sent to the town minister from a company that printed Bibles; the other was addressed to the local mercantile from a firm that marketed seed packets.

Grant and Nora sat across from each other over coffee at the cafe.

"It was a good idea, but it doesn't look as though it got us anywhere," Nora concluded.

Grant dipped his spoon into his coffee and swirled it around several times. "We haven't tried our postmaster yet. After all, Charley did live here once. Maybe Adele's cousin resides in Coltonville."

A smile formed on Nora's face. "We've nothing to lose. We'll need the sheriff. The postmaster won't reveal that information without legal cause."

They found Sheriff Logan in his office and presented him with their idea. He agreed to intervene on their behalf and accompanied them to the post office, where he explained the information he needed to Jeb Hooper. Hooper was tall and lanky. He wore wire-rimmed spectacles that balanced awkwardly on the end of his long nose. He had a way of tilting his head and staring down his nose as though he needed to focus his eyes through his lenses at just the right angle.

"I have an excellent memory, Sheriff, and I can assure you that no letter arrived within the last month, or any other time, bearing the return address of anyone named Ferris. In light of Charley's death, such a missive would have immediately struck my attention."

"What about a letter with a St. Louis postmark?" Nora pressed.

"Now, that's another matter. Let me see . . . there was such a letter addressed to you, Sheriff."

Logan reflected. "Yes, that's right. About two weeks ago, I received a packet from the authorities containing some wanted posters. What else?"

"Steve Collins received such a letter. There was no return address."

"Steve and his sister, Mary, are my closest friends," Grant said. "We've already discussed Charley Ferris, and I can tell you that they know no more about him than we do."

"Joe Crandall received a letter."

Grant and Nora glanced at the sheriff.

Logan nodded. "He's got a ranch east of town," he said by way of explanation.

"His letter had no return address."

"Any others?"

"Only one. Miss Winslow at the millinery received a letter . . . it came from a manufacturer of hats."

Logan frowned. "Then, that leaves Crandall."

Joe Crandall lived about three miles outside of Coltonville. Sheriff Logan explained that he had moved into the area about a year and a half ago. He was quiet, kept to himself, and did not cause any trouble. He rode into town for supplies about once a month. Other than that, Logan admitted to knowing nothing about him.

Grant and Logan rode out to Crandall's spread. It consisted of a modest-looking house and barn, along with some dilapidated outbuildings. There was still a light covering of snow on the ground, and the roofs of each structure were coated in white. A thin plume of smoke rose from the chimney, but other than that, there was no sign of life.

They dismounted and tied their horses to a hitching rail next to the front porch. Sheriff Logan cast a cautious glance around and then stepped onto the porch. He knocked at the door and waited. There was no response. He knocked again and called out. "Mr. Crandall! It's Sheriff Logan." A long silence followed, and Sheriff Logan turned the knob and opened the door. He stepped inside and called out Crandall's name again but there was still no answer. Grant waited by the horses while Logan disappeared inside. A minute later, he emerged. "The table's set and there's coffee on the stove but there's no one inside." Adjusting his gloves, he scanned the ground around the outbuildings.

"There are tracks leading toward the barn," Grant observed.

"Yeah, let's take a look."

Logan had just stepped off the porch when a shot suddenly rang out and whistled past them. They dived to the ground and crawled toward a water trough.

"Where did that shot come from?" Logan asked.

"The barn. I saw the door close."

Logan raised himself on his elbow and peeked around the side of the trough. "Mr. Crandall, if that's you inside the barn, hold your fire. It's Sheriff Logan."

Following a long pause, a voice came from the barn. "You're not wanted here, Sheriff. Ride away and leave me be."

"I need to talk to you, Crandall . . . and I'm not leaving until I do."

The barn door opened an inch and the barrel of a rifle jutted out.

"Hold your fire, Crandall. All I want to do is talk to you."

"I ain't doin' no talkin', Sheriff. Now, this is your last warnin'. I'll hold my fire providin' you mount up and ride out."

Logan shook his head and drew his .45. "Give me some cover, Will. I'll work my way around the barn to the left and try to flank him."

Grant drew his gun and moved along the ground on his elbows until he reached the right side of the trough.

"Now!" Logan directed.

Upon the command, Grant raised his .45 and fired just to the left of the barn door. He saw his bullet splinter the wood and then saw the barn door close. Five seconds later, he fired another round, and then another. He heard Logan running toward the barn and saw him disappear around the side. The barn door opened again, and once more Grant saw the rifle barrel poke through. He fired another round, this time a little closer, and saw a hand reach out and pull the door shut. About thirty seconds later, he heard a muffled shot followed by a thud. The barn door opened, and Logan stepped into view, waving to Grant. Grant got to his feet and made his way to the barn, where he saw a limp form stretched out on the hay.

"Is that Crandall?"

"It is. I had to bend the barrel of my .45 over his head. He very nearly shot me before I did. I must be losing a step in my old age."

Grant holstered his gun and knelt down beside Crandall. "I don't remember ever seeing him before."

"The man's never been one for socializing. Help me get him in the house. We'll get him cleaned up."

Crandall looked to be about fifty. He had a week of black stubble on his face. He was bald except for a ragged line of rank hair around his ears. His clothes were old and worn, and he bore the marks of a man who had given up on life. There was a welt the size of a walnut just above his right ear. Sheriff Logan had placed a wet compress over it. When Crandall finally came around, he moaned, and his hand moved toward the ripe bruise on his head. It took a while for his eyes to focus. When they did, he started to get up from his settee, but he felt the swelling pain and lay down again.

"Well, Mr. Crandall, why did you try to shoot me?" Logan asked as he pushed back his Stetson.

"It was nothin' personal against you, Sheriff. You never done me any harm. I just ain't goin' back."

"Back where?"

"To Kansas."

Logan and Grant glanced at each other.

"What do you mean?"

"Don't be playin' games, Sheriff. I know why you came out here . . . to arrest me. Nobody ever comes out here. I been able to stay hidden for close onto two years now," Crandall said, gritting his teeth in pain as he felt the growing welt on his head. "I knew there were wanted posters still out on me, but I thought I'd done a good job stayin' hidden."

"Tell me about Kansas."

"I got caught up in a range dispute. I burned down a man's house and his barn. Oh, he deserved it all right . . . after what he done to me and others, but . . . well, I ran and I've been on the dodge ever since."

Logan regarded him narrowly for a long moment.

"Crandall, not too long ago, you got a letter postmarked in St. Louis."

Crandall eyed the sheriff in confusion.

"Who sent you that letter?"

"What . . . what are you talkin' about?"

"The postmaster confirmed that you received that letter within the last month."

"Yeah, that's true enough. My sister lives there. She wrote me. She sends me money from time to time . . . to help with the farm. What does my sister have to do with this? Why do you want to know about the letter?"

Logan took a deep breath and let it out slowly as he shot a disappointed glance at Grant.

Grant slumped down heavily in a chair.

"Never mind, Crandall. It's just a misunderstanding," Logan stated.

Crandall shook his head to clear it. "You mean you didn't come out here to arrest me . . . for what I did in Kansas?"

"No. I didn't know anything about Kansas."

Crandall groaned and fell back on the settee, pulling the compress over his eyes.

Grant retired early that night. He was deeply troubled by his failure to locate Adele Ferris' cousin. Since no one had come forward to claim Adele's body, he feared that it would be impossible to learn the identity of her kin. There could be but two reasons for her cousin to remain unidentified. Either he must have been in on the robbery with Charley, or he simply dreaded being linked to Charley for fear that he would be suspected of having some connection with the robbery. Grant opted for the former, for it was simply too much of a coincidence for both Charley and his daughter to have been killed in two separate incidents within so short a period of time. Grant concluded that Adele's own cousin had taken a hand in her death. The final link between Charley and Adele and the cousin was severed. Grant believed that if he could find the cousin, he would find the man who robbed the express office and killed Tom Elsworth. These thoughts occupied his mind over and over again until he was too tired to think any more. Finally, he drifted off to sleep.

Chapter Nine

Several more days had passed, but there was still no response from the St. Louis authorities concerning the identity of Adele Ferris' cousin. Grant was disappointed but not surprised. After all, it had been a long shot from the beginning. If there had been any doubt among the residents of Coltonville as to his guilt, it was assuredly erased when the payroll money showed up again and had passed through his hands. Some of the town merchants would probably be reluctant even to trade with him. He felt deep down that the sheriff, at least, harbored some doubts about his guilt. On the other hand, maybe Logan was operating on the opinion that, given enough rope, he would hang himself.

As far as Nora was concerned, he could not exactly read her intentions. There were times when he sensed within her a confidence in his innocence, yet he may have misconstrued her intentions as a desire to further her own career with a news-breaking story. The hard truth was that there were very few that he could trust, and there was no one who could extricate him from the quicksand in which he was mired. He had to wait . . . wait for the real thief to move again, and he had to be ready. There was one factor that gave him some small measure of satisfaction. Having substituted the express office money for the bills in Grant's cabinet, the real thief must be very curious now as to why Grant was not behind bars at this very minute. That had to create doubt and confusion, and it might be enough to force the thief into action again. It was this on which he was banking.

Grant did not have long to wait. It was early one morning when he thought he heard a noise outside his ranch house. He looked through his kitchen window and saw what he imagined to be a shadow moving near his barn. He lifted his .45 from his holster and slipped outside. The moon was half full but partly obscured by clouds. As so, it cast a milky glow over ground that was already blanketed with scattered pecks of snow. Keeping low, Grant moved cautiously toward the barn, his gun ready if he needed to use it.

When he reached the door, he found the bar still in place. Glancing about, he made a furtive circle around the structure. He saw nothing out of the ordinary. The ground was in no condition to reveal tracks, even if he could read them in the diminishing light. Returning to the door, he removed the bar and entered. He lit the lantern that hung from the nearest post and looked around. The bay was there. Its ears pricked up at the sound of his entry, and it swayed its head to glance in his direction. Slowly, Grant made his way past the stalls. The barn seemed to be intact. He shoved the .45 under his belt, patted the bay on its flank, and returned to the house.

Grant was relieved, yet he wondered about the incident for some time. He was reasonably certain he had heard something, but it could have been an animal prowling about. He thought he had seen a flitting shadow, but he may have been jumping to conclusions due to his state of mind. He decided to remain awake for the rest of the night to watch for any intruder. He made a pot of coffee, placed his .45 on the table, turned off his lamps, and sat in front of the window.

Just after midnight, he heard a lone coyote howling somewhere off in the distance. It served as the only reminder that he was not alone on earth.

Morning came without incident. The cloud bank that had moved in during the night brought with it another inch of snow. If there had been any tracks from the previous evening, they were now obliterated.

Grant stretched out on his settee and decided to sleep for a while. His eyelids were heavy and he felt tired. He rested for a time, but the sound of an approaching horse jarred him awake, and he reached for his .45. Parting the curtain over his window, he saw a figure in a long cloak on his porch. He moved to the door and opened it, his gun still in his hand.

Removing her hood, Nora Masters stood before him, her eyes wide at the sight of his weapon. "Do you always greet guests with a gun?"

"Sorry. I guess I was expecting someone else."

"I see."

He waved her in and tucked the .45 back under his belt.

"You look done in . . . a little unhinged."

Grant ran his hand across the stubble on his face and then pushed his fingers through his tousled hair. "Yeah, I guess I don't look so good."

"I didn't say that," she replied, the corners of her mouth rising in a wry smile.

He grinned. "I was up all night. I thought there was someone or something prowling around my barn, and I was keeping watch."

She eyed him pensively. "I'll fix some coffee," she said as she removed her cloak.

"I'll get cleaned up."

Grant shaved, washed, and changed his shirt. When he returned to the kitchen, Nora was pouring coffee into a pair of cups. The two of them sat down and enjoyed the hot brew.

"How is it?" she asked.

"Good. It's nice to have a woman's touch around the house."

"I couldn't find the sugar."

"The last cupboard on the left."

She opened the cupboard door and removed a canister of sugar. She poured some into a bowl and then spooned a little into her cup. "Do you want some?"

He shook his head.

"You certainly look better," she remarked, considering his face.

"Better compared to what?"

She chuckled.

"What brings you out here?"

She took a piece of paper from her sleeve and pushed it across the table toward him.

Grant picked it up, unfolded it, and examined it. It was a message, printed, in pencil.

IF YOU WANT EVIDENCE OF THE EXPRESS OFFICE ROBBERY, YOU'LL FIND IT ON WILL GRANT THE NEXT TIME HE RIDES INTO TOWN.

The note was unsigned. Grant studied the paper for a full minute before he returned it. "Where did you get this?"

"It was slipped under the door of *The Tribune*. I found it this morning when I came to work."

"And you didn't show it to the sheriff?"

"I didn't even show it to the editor."

"Why not?"

"Are you kidding? This may be the biggest scoop I'll have in years. Besides, it wasn't meant for the sheriff. If it were, it would have been slipped under his door."

"That's a good point. Maybe the person who wrote this thinks the sheriff had his chance to arrest me and didn't. Maybe he thinks the newspaper will put enough pressure on him to act."

"Could be."

"Little does the writer of this note know that it was you who helped to keep me out of jail when those bills turned up."

"Well, one thing's for sure . . . no self-respecting reporter could pass up an opportunity like this. If I don't act on this, someone is going to wonder why."

Grant ran his hand across his chin in thought. "What do you suppose the note means?"

"I was hoping you could tell me."

"That sounds as though you believe that I have the stolen money."

"I didn't say that. I just wanted to give you an opportunity to offer an explanation."

"Suppose I told you that I don't have one?"

She eyed him curiously over the rim of her cup. "Somebody knows something."

"And that somebody is working very hard to make me look guilty. I wonder . . ."

"What is it?"

Suddenly, he climbed to his feet. "Get your cloak."

Two minutes later, they were in the barn. Grant lit the

lantern and looked around. "I thought I saw something out here last night. Maybe I was right after all." He stepped to the first stall and hung the lantern from a nail. He removed his saddle blanket from the top board of the stall and spread it out over the straw. He then hefted his saddlebags and emptied the contents onto the blanket. Among them were a shirt and a spare pair of socks. He went through the pockets of the shirt and turned the socks inside out. He turned over his frying pan, plate, and cup. "There's nothing here." He then began to replace each item. As he picked up his coffeepot, he paused. He shook it but heard nothing. Opening the lid, he turned over the pot and watched a sock fall out. He picked it up and reached inside. From the sock, he withdrew a wad of curled up bills. He glanced at Nora, who was watching him curiously. He counted out the bills as he stacked them on the blanket. "Five hundred . . . in twenties and fifties."

Nora's eyes widened.

Grant examined the sock closely. He turned it over in his hands and held it to his nose. It was then that the bay whinnied softly. Grant looked up. He heard nothing but he sensed someone was near. His hand moved toward his belt for his .45, but in his haste to reach the barn he realized he did not bring it.

"What is it?" Nora asked.

He held his finger to his lips and focused on the barn door. He thought he detected the sound of a footstep. Taking Nora's arm, he pulled her aside and pointed toward the far stall. "Get in there and keep low. Don't make a sound," he whispered.

She nodded and did as he instructed.

Within seconds, a shadow passed over the ground in front of the door. Grant took a deep breath and watched as Karl and Jonas Tarver stepped inside, their rifles in their hands.

"What is it? What do you want here?"

"Shut up, Grant!" Karl rapped.

"You men get off my property, or I'll have the law on you."

Karl sneered. "You . . . will have the law on us? You . . . a thief and a murderer?"

Jonas nudged his brother. "Karl, look . . . over there . . . on the blanket."

Karl's eyes widened as he saw the money. "Pick it up, Jonas."

Jonas did as ordered. "There must be hundreds of dollars here!"

"I didn't know that you could count that high, Jonas," Grant said disdainfully.

"You shut up!" Jonas replied.

"I know your brother can't."

Karl cocked his Winchester and moved a step closer toward Grant. "You're askin' for it, Grant. Just give me a reason."

"It looks as though you have five hundred of them right there."

"Five hundred!" Jonas repeated.

Karl's eyes widened. "We've been out here before . . . when you were in prison. We searched your place but couldn't find nothin'."

"So you were the ones. I understand you left my house in a mess, but then I guess you're used to living in a pigsty."

"You hid it good, all right. Where's the rest of it?"

Grant did not reply.

"I said—"

"I heard you." Grant pushed his hands into his pockets. "Suppose I told you I don't know where the rest is? Suppose I told you I just found this money in my barn?"

Both Karl and Jonas burst out into raucous laughter.

"Yeah, that's how I thought you might react."

Karl stepped closer to Grant and eyed him narrowly. "Now, suppose you tell us where the rest is, and we'll let you ride out."

"I can't. I don't know."

Karl raised his rifle and aimed it squarely at Grant's chest.

"Why don't you boys just take the money and leave. It's a sizable amount. Besides, there's nothing I can do about it. After all, I can't very well go to the sheriff and report that money that I stole was stolen from me."

"He's right, Karl. There's more money here than we've ever seen," Jonas said, stuffing the bills into the pockets of his coat.

Karl considered the logic and slowly came to the same conclusion. "All right, but we'll be watchin' and waitin'.

There won't be any place you can run or hide where we won't be able to run you to ground, and when you pick up the rest . . ."

"I get the picture."

"Let's get, Karl."

Karl nodded. "We'll ride, but before we go we owe you somethin' for that beatin' you gave us in the cafe."

Grant tensed as he watched Karl move closer toward him. He considered making a move but . . . unarmed . . . against two Winchesters . . . the odds were not in his favor.

Karl flashed an uneven row of broken teeth at Grant and then swung out with his rifle butt.

Chapter Ten

When Grant came around, the first thing he saw was Nora. Her hands were soft as they moved tenderly about his face. At first, he could not see her clearly, but after a minute she came into focus. He tried to sit up, but he felt dizzy and fell back on the straw.

"You'd better take it easy. You've got quite a welt on your head."

Grant worked his hand up to his forehead, where he felt a bump the size of a walnut a few inches above his eye. He flinched in pain when he touched it.

"I couldn't find any bandages, but I wet some towels and was able to clear away the blood."

Grant moaned. "How long have I been out?"

"About forty-five minutes, I imagine. I thought, for a

while, that you weren't going to regain consciousness," she said, pressing the towel to his head again.

Slowly, he managed to sit up. He held the towel against his skin for a time before taking it away. "They . . . didn't find you, then?"

"No. The one named Karl hit you, and then they left."

"Well, we know one thing anyway. The Tarvers weren't in on the robbery."

"Did you suspect them?"

"Not really. They're mean enough but they lack the brains."

"What do you plan to do about them?"

"Nothing . . . for now."

"Nothing?"

"I'll mention it to the sheriff, in time, but not just yet."

She shot a puzzled look at him.

"Well, I can't very well report to the law that the express office payroll was in my possession when I was robbed of it, can I?"

"No, I guess not."

"But it seems to me that that works both ways. Sooner or later, the Tarvers are going to spend that money. It might be interesting to see how they explain where they got it. After all, they can't tell the sheriff that they stole it from me."

Nora smiled.

"That takes some of the pressure off me. Besides, it might shake up the real thief. He'll wonder how the

Tarvers got hold of that money after he planted it on me. It may even force him into making another move."

"You're an interesting man, Will Grant," Nora remarked admiringly.

"Right now, all I feel is sore. You might have to help me into the house."

She took his arm as he struggled to his feet. He reeled to his left, but she uprighted him and they struggled back to the house. Nora braced him all the way until he collapsed onto the settee.

"I'll go for the doctor," she said.

"No, I'm sure I'll be all right . . . once this dizziness clears."

"I don't feel good about leaving you alone like this."

"I'm not planning on going anywhere."

"I'll get you a blanket."

"The bedroom is in there," he said, nodding with his head.

She returned in a moment and dropped a blanket over him. "I'll be back this afternoon. If you're no better by then, I'm going to take you into town to see the doctor."

"Fair enough. One more thing before you go . . . my gun . . . over there. Let me have it."

She picked up the .45 and handed it to him.

He tucked it under the blanket.

"I'll wet another towel for you before I leave," she said.

His eyes were closed when she gently laid the towel across his forehead.

"Thanks," he said, extending his hand.

She took it and squeezed it. She then left, closing the door behind her as quietly as she could.

Grant did not know how long he had lain on the settee. All he knew was that his head felt like a piece of kindling that had been split by an axe. He slept on and off, and in time, his dizziness waned. He was concerned that it would return, however, if he sat up. He was almost afraid to attempt it but he finally did. Fortunately, he was all right. Even his focus seemed to be normal. He sat up for a long time, not wanting to press his luck by climbing to his feet. The clock on the mantle read just after two o'clock. He wondered if it was afternoon or morning. A glance toward the window told him that it was still daylight.

Shortly, he heard the sound of a horse. "A buggy," he said to himself. He reached for the .45 and cradled it on his lap under the blanket. There was a light tap on the door, and he called out, "Come in."

The door opened and Nora entered. She carried a basket, which she set on the table. "How are you feeling?" she asked, a look of concern on her face.

"Better, I think."

She loosened her cloak and hung it on a wall peg. She then opened the basket and removed a bottle and some bandages. She sat next to him on the settee and ran her hand over his forehead. "I brought some disinfectant. I'm going to clean your wound and dress it."

He nodded and settled back while she opened the bottle. The tincture had a strong odor and it burned when she dabbed his forehead with it. He winced and gritted his teeth as she seemed to take forever to finish.

"I'm sure this hurts but I'm just about done." She corked the bottle and proceeded to bandage his head. When she was done, she stood up and looked at her work with a critical eye.

Grant slid his hand over the bandage. The construction felt awkward, but somehow he was glad it was there.

"Can you eat something?"

"I don't know. I guess I'm hungry."

"I'll wash up and set the table."

Within minutes, she had things going in the kitchen. She fired up the stove and then prepared the table. She removed a canister from her basket and poured the contents into a pot, which she set on the stove. Soon, she had everything ready, and the pleasant aromas of coffee and beef mingled together to transform the atmosphere of the kitchen into something wonderful. She helped Grant to his feet and steered him toward the table. He felt reasonably stable and concluded that he would have been able to walk without assistance.

"I hope you like beef stew," she said, standing beside him and filling his cup with steaming coffee.

"I love it." He picked up his spoon, dipped it into his bowl, and removed a piece of meat and a fragment of potato. He blew on it for a moment, sampled it, and then smiled. "It's the best stew I ever tasted. You're a great cook."

She smiled. "I wish I could take credit for it, but I picked it up at the cafe."

"Why did you tell me? I wouldn't have known the difference."

"The integrity of a reporter," she replied with a smile that showed a nice row of white teeth.

He smiled back.

"I'm sorry that the cornbread isn't warm."

"It's a fine meal. Thank you."

She took a spoonful of stew and chewed it carefully for some time. "I thought you might be interested in knowing that one of the Tarvers has been arrested already."

Grant's eyes widened. "Which one?"

"The slower-witted one."

"Which one would that be?"

She smirked. "Jonas, I think. He was flashing money around the saloon. The bartender got suspicious and reported it to Sheriff Logan. Well, to make a long story short, Jonas is now in jail."

"What about Karl?"

"The sheriff was looking for him when I left town. Oh, and it might please you to know that Jonas resisted arrest. Sheriff Logan knocked him out with the barrel of his .45."

Grant grinned. "Somehow, that does make me feel better. In fact, it eases my pain considerably."

Nora pushed her plate aside and folded her hands on the table in front of her. "Don't you have any idea at all who robbed the express office and framed you?"

It was a question that took him by surprise. "Does that mean that you believe in my innocence?"

"Let's just say that I like to keep an open mind."

"Well, that's fair enough."

She stared at him for a long moment. "Well, do you suspect someone?"

"I didn't at the time of my arrest but I do now."

"Who?" she asked, her eyes wide with curiosity.

"I'd rather not say just yet because I may be wrong."

"But—"

"I spent a year of my life behind bars because I was misjudged. I don't want to do the same thing to someone else."

She regarded him closely with, what Grant construed to be, admiration. "What, then, do you plan to do about your suspicions?"

"As soon as this drum stops pounding in my head, I'll make my play."

"Of course. You're still not back to normal. If I can be of any help, let me know."

"I'll do that."

"You do trust me, don't you?"

He considered her question before answering. "You helped me when I needed help, and you remained silent about the anonymous note you received and the money that was planted in my barn. If you were only interested in a story for your paper, you would've already written it. Yes, I trust you."

She smiled. "Are you saying that you owe me an interview?"

"Maybe."

She shrugged. "Well, I suppose a 'maybe' is better than nothing." She stood up. "I'd better be going. You'll be all right by yourself?"

"I think so."

She placed her hand on his shoulder. "Take care of yourself."

"Thanks for the dinner."

He watched her don her cloak and step through the door. As she rode away in her buggy, he thought about her for a long time. He hoped that he was right in his assessment of her.

Grant napped off and on for the rest of the day. He felt rocky and decided to stay inside. Too shaky to ride, he realized that even a short trip might set him back. He did not feel hungry again after eating the stew that Nora had brought, but he did drink plenty of water and made some fresh coffee, which he sipped throughout the evening.

Late in the evening, his head still pounding, Grant sat by the fireplace and tried to sort out his thoughts. Once again, he took up paper and pencil and roughed out a sketch of the express office. For the first time in a year, however, he looked at the sketch differently, and he was deeply troubled by the conclusions that he drew. For a long time, he stared at the paper. Finally, he crumpled it up and threw it into the fire, watching it burn to cinders before his eyes. He continued to stare blindly at the dancing flames for the better part of an hour, clutching the arms of his chair from time to time in anger and frustration.

It was late when he retired to his bed, but the mattress somehow felt uncomfortable, and he found himself returning to the settee in the parlor. Here, he sat up most of the night with the blanket wrapped around him, experiencing what seemed like a hundred dreams, and sleeping what felt like minutes instead of hours.

Nora walked into the office of *The Tribune* and hung up her cloak. She smiled at Mr. Creighton, the editor, who was at his desk laboring over a stack of papers.

"Good morning, Mr. Creighton."

"Morning, Nora."

Ben, the typesetter, flashed a smile at her as he moved about his work station.

"Good morning, Ben."

A wisp of a man, Ben touched the brim of his green visor and said, "Mornin' Miss Nora."

"How's the column on the express office robbery coming?" Creighton asked.

Nora shrugged as she slipped behind her typewriter. "Not too well."

Creighton's brow furrowed as he stared at her over his tiny spectacles.

"You know, Mr. Creighton, this job isn't exactly what I expected it to be."

Creighton stood up, pressed his hands into the small of his back, and then stepped over to Nora's desk. He was about seventy, small of build, and a bit hunched. His gray hair was receding, and the skin was drawn so tightly across his face that he looked gaunt. He was the kind of man one would enjoy taking to a restaurant for a T-bone steak. "Most jobs aren't what we expect them to be—even the simplest ones. Putting out a newspaper is a bit more complicated than most."

"I have to admit that I thought it would be more glamorous. I envisioned seeing my name in a byline on a regular basis and receiving the respect of everyone in town."

"You've done a credible job so far. Some folks will respect you; others won't. That part of the job is like any other. As far as the notoriety is concerned . . . well, only time will tell how far anyone will go in any given profession."

She frowned as she stared blankly at the top of her desk.

Sensing her mood, he said, "You're young. I'm old. I've been in this profession most of my life. I don't rightly know anything else. I started as a boy back East when I ran errands and sold papers on the street. I've done a little bit of everything from selling ads, to taking photographs, to writing, to editing. I've been punched in the mouth and pelted with stones. Once, back in Boston, the editor and I had to run for our lives when an angry mob destroyed our office and set fire to our equipment. It's all part of the business."

"Then, why do you do it?"

He cast a knowing smile. "It gets in your blood, I guess. There's a special feeling you get when you put out a paper. I still get it to this very day. It's kind of a noble cause—as though you're serving a purpose. There's a real need for expressing the truth to the public . . . for showing both sides of an issue. The people have to be made aware of the facts. It makes for a better community. It makes for a stronger country."

Nora regarded him with admiration. "That's a very good way of looking at things. You're a wise man, Mr. Creighton."

He allowed himself a small grin.

"It makes me ashamed that I feel so defeated. It's just that I want everyone to know the truth, but I'm not getting anywhere in my attempts. I've had people ignore me, slam doors in my face, lie to me."

"Nobody said that finding the truth was easy. Sometimes you have to dig for it, and sometimes you even have to blast—like a miner going through rock."

"It's much more of a people job than I thought it would be, and it's hard to be able to read people accurately."

Creighton adjusted his spectacles. "This Will Grant business getting you down, is it?"

She nodded.

"Well, you certainly spent enough time researching it."

"I've read and reread everything that you wrote about

it a year ago. I've interviewed as many people connected with the case as would talk to me. The facts seem to be right, yet there's still something missing."

"Then, you have to dig deeper."

"I don't really know what else to do."

"Have you gotten your interview with Grant yet?"

"I've spoken to him on a number of occasions, but he really hasn't confided in me."

"Do you like him?"

Taken aback by the directness of the question, Nora hesitated. "Yes, I do."

"I like him as well. Have you formed an opinion about the matter?"

"In part, yes, but a gut feeling isn't the same as being able to prove anything."

"Some questions can't be answered. All stories don't have endings."

"The end of this story has to be told—for Will Grant's sake . . . for the town's sake."

Creighton pulled a handkerchief from his back pocket and wiped his spectacles. Considering Nora closely, he said, "It's not a reporter's job to solve old cases. It's your duty to report the facts, to show all sides, and let the reader draw his own conclusions."

"And, if during the course of my research I come to believe that an injustice has been done, do I do nothing about it because I can't get answers?"

"It's perfectly fine to raise questions, but there's no place for a reporter's personal feelings in a newspaper. We have an obligation to deal in facts, and the facts should never be slanted to reflect our opinions. Report the facts as they fall. In that sense, your job is an easy one."

Nora knew exactly what Mr. Creighton meant; what was more, she knew he was right. Yet she also knew that she was walking a tightrope.

Chapter Eleven

Grant awoke the following morning with a headache. The skin around the bump on his skull felt as though it had been stretched tightly, like a wet strip of rawhide. He moved his fingers to his head, but he forgot about the bandage that Nora had fastened there. He sat up and rolled his legs over the edge of the bed, allowing his feet to touch the floor. He felt all right. He stood up, bracing himself against an end table. He did not need the support. The dizziness was gone and he could focus clearly. He dressed and made his way into the kitchen, where he lit a fire in the stove. He made coffee and then, while the pot was heating, he moved into the parlor, where he added some logs to the fireplace. Soon, he had a hearty blaze going. For breakfast, he decided to finish the beef stew Nora had brought him yesterday. He set to work in the kitchen, preparing the meal, sipping coffee as he worked. In no time at all, the house was filled again with the pleasant aromas of beef, carrots, potatoes, and coffee. Grant could hardly wait to eat as he ladled the stew onto his plate and set it on the table. He quickly consumed the entire bowl and had enough remaining in the pot for half of another bowl. He topped off the last morsel with a second cup of coffee and then leaned back in his chair, satisfied and full.

He cleaned the table, washed and shaved, strapped on his .45, and made his way to the barn. The bay looked his way when he opened the barn door and entered. He patted down the horse and led it out of the stall. As Grant reached for the bay's blanket, he heard a familiar sound—the cocking of a rifle. He turned slowly and saw Karl Tarvar standing just inside the door, a Winchester cradled in his hands.

"Well, Karl, I'm a little surprised to see you back here. What more do you want?"

"I want the rest of it."

"The rest of what?"

"Don't play games with me, Grant, or I'll put a bullet in your gut this time and watch you bleed to death here in your own barn."

Grant took a deep breath and slowly released it. "Look, Karl, I don't suppose it would do any good to—"

The expression on Tarver's face hardened. "I don't have much time, Grant. The law's already got my brother in a cell, and they're hot on my trail. I'm aimin' to leave the territory, and I need money—big money—and you're the only one who can give it to me."

Grant considered tossing the horse blanket at Tarver and making a play for his .45, but he quickly concluded that the odds against such a maneuver were too long.

"It won't do you any good denyin' you have the money. The five hundred we took from you proves you've got it. I'll leave half of it for you, but I need the rest for a stake . . . else neither one of us will live to spend it."

Grant knew that it would be pointless to dispute the matter with Tarver. After all, the five hundred dollars did make him look guilty. He could not fault Tarver for drawing the conclusion that he did. He decided to go along with Tarver in an effort to buy some time. Perhaps on the trail he would be able to overpower Tarver or escape from him. "All right, Karl. You've got it right this time. I do have it."

A grin of satisfaction curled Tarver's lips.

"But it's not here."

"Where is it?"

"My partner has it . . . in town."

Tarver eyed him narrowly.

Grant was not certain that Tarver would buy his story, but he knew that Tarver was as desperate as he was—in his own way. Besides, it was his only chance.

Finally, Tarver nodded. "All right, we'll wait until dark. Then, we'll take us a ride, but if you're lyin' . . . I'll be headin' west with an extra horse."

Grant bit his lower lip.

"Loosen your gun belt and toss it in the hay—careful like."

Grant did as he was ordered.

"Now, we'll just mosey on in to your house. You can fix me some grub and—" Tarver's eyes bulged out as he suddenly gasped for air. The Winchester fell from his hands as he sank to his knees. Slowly, he pitched forward onto his face, a knife protruding from his back.

Grant stared at Tarver in disbelief, not realizing that he was holding his breath. He watched Tarver's right hand constrict in pain, his fingers tightly clutching the straw on the floor of the barn. Within seconds, Tarver relaxed his grip and he did not move again. Grant exhaled. He heard footsteps. Glancing up, he saw the strangest looking man he had ever encountered. Barely five feet tall, he seemed slight in build despite his bulky red coat. His long, straight white hair gave his round face a boyish appearance, yet his wrinkled skin suggested an age of at least forty. His eyes were colorless, his face beyond pale as though he had never seen the light of the sun. The man eyed Grant carefully as he stepped up to Tarver's body and jerked the knife free. Using a clump of straw, he wiped the blood from the blade and then inserted the knife into his boot.

"Hello, Will." The voice came from somewhere outside.

Grant gazed toward the door. A few seconds later,

a man entered. He was tall and lean and sported a thin mustache. He wore a dark Stetson and a rawhide-colored coat. Grant recognized him at once as Joe Welker, a fellow inmate. He served five years for bank robbery and was released just a month before Grant was freed.

"Hello, Joe. I'm surprised to see you in these parts. I thought you were headed west."

"I got sidetracked—by an interesting newspaper article about a man."

Grant considered Welker closely.

"It seems that a man was murdered . . . a man who claimed that he had a part in the robbery of an express office—the express office that you were accused of robbing. I heard about your release, and I thought I'd drop by for a visit." Welker's hooded eyes focused hard on Grant as he stepped forward, his hands buried deep in his pockets.

Grant nodded his understanding.

"You know, it's a funny thing, Will . . . back in the pen I always thought you were innocent. Most of the cons did. You just weren't the kind of man who would commit such a crime. Imagine my surprise when I overheard your conversation with this man . . . Karl, I believe you called him."

"I was bluffing about the money, Joe, in order to buy time. I truly had nothing to do with that robbery, but there are still plenty of people around here who think I did."

Welker grinned. "I've been around town for a while

now, Will. I heard about that money from the robbery that turned up within days after your return—money that hasn't seen the light of day since you went to prison."

"If I had stolen that payroll, do you think I would be fool enough to spend it as soon as I was released from prison?"

"I wouldn't think so but something is going on, and whatever it is you're the key."

"Look, Joe—"

"Save your breath, Will. I know all about the money that this man's brother was flashing. The sheriff took him into custody but this one was smarter. He slipped away."

"But you followed him."

"I followed him, and where do you think he led me— right here to your spread. For a while, I thought he and his brother might have been your partners, but after overhearing your conversation, I know otherwise."

Grant remembered Welker well. He was an opportunist, a confidence man, and a sneak. Behind bars, he was nicknamed the 'ferret.' Grant had never mixed with him that much, but during confinement, proximity and isolation from the outside world lead to a certain exchange among convicts. Such a thing was only natural. Grant never regarded Welker as vicious, but he did mark him as a man on whom he would never turn his back. Clever, cunning, and conniving, Welker could smell out a dollar the way a coyote could sniff out a prairie dog. Grant quickly concluded that there was no sense in arguing with Welker. The circumstances were such that he would never convince the man of the truth. Within the last five minutes, nothing had changed for him except that now he had two men with whom to contend instead of one.

"The deal that you made with your friend here is still in place. The only difference is that now there's a three-way split. A third for you, a third for me, and a third for Lugo. Oh, forgive my manners. I neglected to introduce my colleague . . . Lugo."

Grant regarded the little man with curiosity.

Lugo, in turn, said nothing. He merely eyed Grant with an interest that made their introduction an awkward one.

"Does Lugo talk?"

"Only when he has something meaningful to say."

Grant nodded.

"Lugo and I were acquaintances before I went to prison. We met while I was . . . shall we say . . . hiding out in the circus. Lugo is a bit of an acrobat . . . and an expert with a knife. He made quite a good living for several years silhouetting the form of a shapely woman with his cutlery—until there was an accident, that is."

Grant glanced at Tarver's body. "Yes, I can see Lugo's work."

"Oh, that's nothing . . . merely child's play. Lugo is far more skillful than that. Show him, Lugo. The knot in that post over there."

Lugo moved a step to his left, reached somewhere behind his neck, and produced three knives. Without even appearing to take aim, he launched all three weapons in such rapid succession that Grant saw nothing but a blur. Grant heard three soft thuds, turned and eyed the post. The knives were embedded around the knot in such close proximity one would be hard pressed to place a nickel within the blades.

Lugo wasted no time in stepping over to the post, removing the knives, and secreting them under the collar of his coat.

"I'm impressed," Grant replied.

Sneering, Welker said, "Most people are. Lugo is handy to have around, and he's quite loyal. Now, suppose we get started."

"What about him?" Grant asked, pointing at Tarver.

"He won't be going anywhere."

"No, I suppose not."

"Get mounted. It's time we met your partner."

Grant did as he was told. As he tightened the cinch on his saddle, he noticed that Lugo was watching him closely, his boyish appearance concealing what must be a particularly cold-blooded individual with the skills of an assassin. Tarver would have been hard enough to handle, but Welker and Lugo together made his odds of escaping too remote even to contemplate. As he swung into the saddle, he began to weigh his possibilities.

Chapter Twelve

The ride into town was a grim one. Joe Welker rode beside Grant, and Lugo trailed some twenty feet behind. With his .45 back in the barn, Grant felt naked against these men. Any type of a showdown was impossible; furthermore, Lugo's speed and accuracy with a knife were enough to dissuade him from any attempt at escape. His only recourse was to manufacture a plan before they reached Coltonville. His comment to Karl Tarver about riding into town to recover his share of the stolen payroll may have painted him into a corner. It was all he could think of at the time. He knew that Karl would balk at returning to town, where he was wanted by the law. Welker, on the other hand, was a free man. Riding down Main Street posed no threat to him. He could, if he chose, stick to Grant like a third arm. Grant concluded that his only hope was to concoct a viable story that would convince Welker and, at the same time, create for himself an opportunity to escape. His time to enact such a plan came sooner than he expected.

When they were on the outskirts of town, Welker grabbed the reins of Grant's horse and drew it to a halt. "All right, before we go any farther, suppose you tell me exactly where in town this money is stashed."

Grant looked at him and frowned.

"Well?"

"I don't know exactly."

Welker's face hardened. "What kind of game are you playing?"

"It's no game. My partner's got the money. He's had it ever since the robbery."

Welker looked at him askance. "Your partner's dead."

"One of them is. There were three of us in on the robbery. One stayed on here in Coltonville. The other lived in Ridley."

"That's the reason you rode over there a while back?"

"You know about that, do you?"

"I know everything about you."

"His name was Charley Ferris."

"I read all about him."

"I kept my mouth shut during the trial and went to prison alone. I guess Charley figured that he owed me something for that. Before he died, he cleared me."

"And your partners didn't spend any of the money while you were behind bars? Do you expect me to believe that?"

"Before we committed the robbery, we agreed to wait a full year before we spent any of it. That's why none of it surfaced before now."

Welker passed his hand across his mouth as he considered Grant's story. "How is it that you don't have your share of the money?"

"When I returned, my partner was ready to give me my share, but I knew there were plenty of people who still believed I was guilty—like the Tarver brothers. I knew there would be plenty, looking over my shoulder, waiting for their chance. That's why I just took what I needed for a while. The Tarvers got that but the rest is still safe—in my partner's hands."

"It looks like you made the right decision."

"Did I? You're here, aren't you?"

Welker sneered. "Yeah, but unlike Karl, I'm willing to leave you with some money in your pocket . . . and your life . . . if you play your cards right."

"Karl promised to leave me half."

"Did you really believe him?"

"No, but then I don't believe you either."

"Well, let's just call it a gesture of faith, from one con to another."

"It doesn't look as though I have much choice."

"You don't have any choice, but you know one thing for sure—if you try to cross me, I'll kill you."

Grant turned and glanced at Lugo, who looked awkward sitting on his horse, his lifeless eyes fixed on Grant.

"That's right. If I don't get you, Lugo will," Welker said, as though he knew what Grant was thinking.

"I get your point."

"All right, before we ride into town, I want to know who your partner is."

"I don't think so."

Welker's hand drifted toward his holster.

Now it was Grant's turn to grin. "If I tell you his name, you could kill me here and now and deal with my partner. No, I plan to stay alive as long as I can. The only insurance I have is keeping my partner's name secret."

"Look, Grant, you're in no position to—"

"What are you worried about? You've got my gun. You've got the drop on me. I'm not going anywhere."

Welker sifted through Grant's words. "All right, but don't suppose that just because we're in town you can cross me. There are plenty of alleys, and as you've seen, Lugo can silence a man very quickly."

"I imagine that Lugo feels comfortable in an alley . . . along with the other rats."

Welker grinned. He released Grant's reins and nodded for him to ride on.

Grant urged the bay onward, uncertain as to his next move. He considered that he may have entrapped himself with the story he had concocted, but he had been unable to create a better one on the spur of the moment. As he led Welker down the main street of town, he

glanced at each building and every passerby in the hope
that something would occur to him . . . something that
would enable him to devise a credible tale that would
satisfy the situation without jeopardizing anyone else.
He knew that Welker was cunning and would not easily
be deceived; he could sense Lugo's quiet presence behind him, ready to cut loose against him at any moment
with his armory of knives. It took precious minutes, but
finally a plan began to form in the back of his mind, and
he quickly realized what his best option—perhaps his
only option—would be.

A small cluster of men was idling in front of the saloon. Not far down the street, he saw Red Morris sort-
ing some tools in a barrel in front of his mercantile.
Grant rode past them until he reached the sheriff's office. It was here that he reined in his mount and turned
to face Welker.

The ex-con gave him a curious look as his eyes
scanned the sign over the door. "Why are we stopping
here?"

"Because this is where my partner is."

Welker scrutinized the street before he turned in his
saddle and glanced at Lugo, who sat on his horse in silence, wearing the same inscrutable expression on his
face.

"Your partner's in jail?"

"No."

"Then—"

"My partner's the law."

"What the—"

"Ken Logan, the sheriff of Coltonville, is my partner."

Welker's jaw suddenly tightened in anger. "Just what are you trying to pull?"

"It's the truth. Logan and I were in on the robbery. He did his best to cover for me at the time, but even he couldn't do much, considering I was found at the scene with a gun in my hand."

Welker stared incredulously at Grant, unable to respond.

"The stolen money has been turning up around town. If you've been following the talk in Coltonville, as you claim, then you know about that."

Welker nodded.

"Well, you have to admit—it does make me look bad—just being out of prison a short time. How do you think I've managed to stay out of the Coltonville jail? Because Logan has covered for me. Whenever anyone pressed him about arresting me, he insisted that I was a free man in the eyes of the law, and he wanted to be careful not to make the same mistake twice. Oh, he had me hauled in for questioning, just to make it look good. There was even a reporter present from the newspaper. Logan claimed that the money could have passed through my hands the same as anybody else's. Officially, he's still investigating the case, and that's the way it stands."

"And the town is buying that?"

Grant shrugged. "Some are . . . some aren't, but the bottom line is that Logan is still in charge, and he carries enough respect around here to pull it off."

Welker lowered his head in thought.

Grant knew that he had the ex-con nearly convinced. He decided to press home his advantage. "When the Tarvers came along and took part of the payroll money from me . . . well, it shifted the blame in another direction. They couldn't very well claim that they stole the five hundred dollars from me. The Tarvers provided us with the break we were looking for. It might've been enough, too, until you had Lugo kill Karl Tarver."

Welker stared at Grant in silence for a long moment, digesting his remarks.

Grant decided to prod him. "Well, do we go in, or do we just sit out here in the cold?"

Welker glanced furtively up and down the street until his beady eyes settled on the door to the sheriff's office. "I'm an ex-con. I don't mix too well with lawmen— even crooked ones."

Grant turned and eyed Lugo. "What about him? Does he have anything to say, or is he just a silent partner?"

"Lugo isn't too comfortable around law dogs either."

"Then, what exactly does this do to our arrangement?"

Welker regarded him bitterly. "Lugo and I will be around." He tugged at his reins and rode off down the street. Lugo followed, occasionally peering over his shoulder in Grant's direction.

Grant shivered as he watched the ghostly figure of

Lugo disappear down a side street near the livery. Breathing a deep sigh of relief, he took a moment to congratulate himself. He had no idea he could be such a convincing liar. He dismounted, tied his horse to the hitching rail, and entered the sheriff's office.

Logan was not there. Grant poured himself a cup of coffee and waited. About ten minutes later, the sheriff walked in.

"Hello, Sheriff."

"Howdy, Will," Logan said as he hung his sheepskin coat from a peg. "What brings you into town?"

"I heard you were looking for Karl Tarver."

"That's right."

"You can stop looking."

Logan eyed him narrowly.

"He's at my place."

Logan pulled some manacles from one of his desk drawers.

"You won't need those."

Logan's eyes widened. "You kill him?"

"No. A character by the name of Lugo is your man. He rides with an ex-con I knew in the pen named Joe Welker."

Logan nodded. "I know the pair. They've been idlin' about town for a couple of weeks now. The small one's a sight to behold."

"I just left their company, or I should say . . . they left mine. I don't imagine they'll be spending any more time in Coltonville."

"Suppose you tell me about it," Logan said, taking the chair behind his desk.

Grant removed his Stetson and dropped it on a side table. He sat down heavily in the nearest chair, folded his arms, and began at the beginning.

Twenty minutes later, Grant stood up and put on his Stetson. "Well, that's about it, Sheriff."

"That's an interesting story."

"I thought you'd enjoy it."

"Which way was Welker headed?"

"East."

"Probably headed for King City. I'll wire the sheriff . . . have him and his partner picked up."

"You'd best warn the sheriff about the small one. He packs more cutlery than the hotel kitchen, and he knows how to use it."

Logan made a note. "I'll send my deputy out to your place to pick up Karl's body. Will you be there?"

"No. I have another errand . . . one that I don't have much desire to run."

"Oh?"

"I'll tell you about it in good time."

He left the office and mounted the bay. As he rode down the street, he heard his name called. Reining in, he turned and saw Steve Collins hastening along the boardwalk.

"Hello, Will."

"Steve."

"Mary asked about you. She said if I saw you, I was to ask you to dinner again."

"As it is, I was planning on riding out to your place today to see her."

"Oh, she's not at home. She rode out to the Danvers spread. Sarah gave birth to twins, and Mary's gone over to help out. She'll be back the day after tomorrow."

Grant nodded.

"Say, what happened to your head?"

"I'll see her then."

Nora made her way down the boardwalk and entered the office of *The Tribune*. She hung her coat on the tree hook and stepped over to her desk. Deep in thought, it took her a moment before she realized that the office was dark. As she glanced about, she noticed that not only were the lamps unlit but the shades were drawn over the front windows.

"Ben . . . Ben, where are you?" she called out to the typesetter.

There was no answer. In fact, the office was deserted. Mr. Creighton, the editor, was out of town, but Ben always remained in the office unless he was at lunch, and it was well past the noon hour. Nora made her way to the back room and opened the door.

"Ben, are you in here?"

The back room was also dark. As soon as she took a step inside, she felt something hard clamp down on her mouth. Her arms were wrenched behind her and held in a viselike grip. She struggled for a moment, in vain, before she realized that it was no use. The door closed behind her. Within seconds, she heard a scratch and saw the harsh glare of a match. It revealed the dark shape of a man—a man she did not know but thought she had seen around town. He lit a lamp and stepped toward her.

"My name is Joe Welker. The one who has you in his grip is my colleague, Lugo."

Nora squirmed in fear but the hands that held her closed even tighter.

"In a moment, Lugo is going to release you. When he does, I want you to sit in this chair. I can promise that no harm will come to you as long as you do what I say."

Nora's eyes widened as she stared at Welker in terror.

"If you scream, Lugo will be forced to cut you. Do you understand?"

Nora nodded.

"All right, Lugo."

The man restraining her released his grip on her mouth first. Then, he slowly let go of her arms and urged her forward.

Nora turned and looked at Lugo. She was startled by his appearance. Rubbing her shoulder, she did as directed and sat down in the chair. "Where is Ben? What have you done with him?"

Welker nodded toward the far corner of the room.

Nora gasped as she saw Ben lying there, his head resting on his outstretched arm.

"He's not seriously hurt . . . just knocked out. He'll come around in a while."

"He's an old man."

"And he should live many more years."

"What is it you want?"

"I want the money that Will Grant stole from the express office."

Nora stared at him in surprise. "Why come to me?"

"I've been in town for a while now. I can see what's going on. You've been spending quite a bit of time with Grant—even more than his girlfriend."

"I'm a reporter. It's my assignment."

"Reporters have a way of learning things. It's their nature. I want to know exactly what it is that you've learned since you've been on your—assignment."

Nora considered the question. "I've come to believe that he's an innocent man."

Welker grinned. "Did you hear that, Lugo?"

Lugo did not reply. He merely continued to stare icily at Nora.

"You're either a very bad reporter or an excellent liar."

"What do you mean? What is it that you know about Will Grant?"

"I know quite a bit about him. I did time with him."

Nora regarded him with surprise.

"I also know that Grant stole that payroll. He admitted it to me."

"I don't believe you."

"Not only did he admit it, but he revealed his partner in the robbery—your sheriff."

Nora remained silent while she tried to digest Welker's words. She knew that his claim was an incredible one. Even if it were true—which she doubted— why would Grant share such information with Welker? "You seem to know more than I do about the matter. Why do you need me?"

"Grant has an 'in' with the sheriff. He knows I can't go near him as long as he's partnered up with the law."

"But you think I can?"

"You seem to be chummy with him. If you learn something that might give me an edge . . . well, I wouldn't object to cutting you in for a percentage."

"What about the sheriff?"

"As a last resort, Lugo and I can deal with him, but only as a last resort, and only after I know where the money is."

Nora felt cornered. She knew that she could never agree to such an arrangement, but if she refused . . . "I . . . I don't know exactly what I can do."

"When the time comes, you will. Think it over. We'll be back, and the next time we meet, have something useful to tell me." He pulled a cheroot from his pocket, struck a match on his thumb, and lit it. He blew smoke into the dimly lit room as he considered her closely. Finally, he slipped through the door, with Lugo at his heels.

Nora breathed a sigh of relief. She quickly moved to

Ben's side and turned him over. She felt a pulse, but his breathing seemed faint.

Thirty minutes later, Ben was resting peacefully in the doctor's office. Nora was seated in the waiting room, and Sheriff Logan was listening to her story.

"Will Grant told me about these boys. The small one—Lugo—killed Karl Tarver," Logan explained.

"What?"

"My deputy brought in his body not too long ago. I had it figured that Welker and Lugo would be on their way out of town, but it appears that greed has overridden their judgement. I'll organize a search and we'll run 'em to ground, sure enough. In the meantime, I'll assign a man to watch you."

She nodded. "Thanks, Sheriff."

Chapter Thirteen

Nora was still a little uneasy the following morning. She decided to stick close to town until Welker and Lugo were picked up. She had breakfast in the hotel dining room and then went directly to the doctor's office to inquire about Ben. Dr. Bailey told her that he was progressing fine but that he wanted to keep him under observation for the next twenty-four hours. Nora felt better about that. She decided not to go to the newspaper office. With Mr. Creighton out of town and Ben at the doctor's office, it meant that she would be alone. Instead, she chose to work in her hotel room. She had lunch at the cafe and then made a trip to the sheriff's office. Deputy Orr was in charge. He informed her that Sheriff Logan was out leading the posse in search of Welker and Lugo. At one point as she was walking about town, she spotted a man wearing a badge. He seemed to be watching her closely. It was then that she recalled Logan had told her that he would have a man keeping an eye on her. His presence made her feel better.

Just before dusk, Nora returned to Dr. Bailey's office to look in on Ben once more. The old typesetter was sitting up in bed and appeared to be feeling much better. Nora helped serve him some broth and then chatted with him for the better part of an hour. She left the doctor's office and crossed over to the cafe, where she had a light dinner. She shunned any company, for she had some thinking to do. Her article on Will Grant was taking shape, but there was still something missing in her story. She had no satisfactory ending. She paid for her meal and then started back toward the hotel, where she planned to work in her room for another hour or so before retiring for the night. There was a slight wind, and the boardwalk was still icy from the last snow. She stepped carefully, keeping her eyes on the path ahead of her in order to avoid slipping in the waning light.

When Nora reached the end of the block, she suddenly saw a pair of legs planted before her, obstructing her path. Looking up, she found herself face to face with Lugo. The dim light from the nearest lamppost cast an eerie glow over his pale skin and left his colorless eyes in deep shadows. So startled was she by his otherworldly appearance, Nora started to scream, but a hand quickly closed over her mouth. She was half-lifted, half-dragged off the boardwalk and into the darkness of the alley, where the familiar voice of Welker whispered in her ear. "I told you we'd be back, Miss Masters. Lugo and I don't give up that easily."

Nora struggled to free herself but could do nothing against his overpowering grip.

"I know the law is out looking for us but that won't stop us. There's too much at stake. You've had time to find out about the payroll. We want answers, and we want them now."

Nora strained to speak, but Welker's hand effectively muffled her words.

"When I remove my hand, speak in a whisper only. I can assure you that I can hear very well. Nod if you understand."

Nora nodded.

"If you attempt to raise an alarm, Lugo will slit your throat in one second."

At that, as if by magic, a long-bladed knife appeared in Lugo's hand.

Nora's eyes widened.

Slowly, Welker slipped his hand away from her mouth. "Now, what have you found out?"

"You were right," Nora spoke softly. "I now believe that Will Grant did take the money."

"I knew it! I knew it! Did you hear that, Lugo?" Welker exclaimed excitedly. straining to keep his own voice in a whisper.

Lugo's expression did not change.

"Where is it?"

"I don't know."

Welker's grip tightened, the leverage pulling her left arm higher and higher until she was standing on her toes to reduce the pressure.

"But I'm working on it. I can find out but I need more time."

"I think you're lying, Miss Masters. You're playing both ends against the middle."

"No, I tell you—"

"You're an attractive woman. Even in this light I can see your large eyes. I can feel the texture of your skin. It's very fine. Your features are exceptionally pleasing to a man, but I can promise you that you won't be anything to look at when Lugo gets through with you. The ugliest man on earth won't want to look at you."

"Please, I'm telling the truth."

"I don't think so, Miss Masters."

Nora's left arm was pinned so far behind her back, it pained her to move it even a fraction of an inch, but she had some degree of freedom with her right arm. Slowly, she moved her hand toward her coat pocket, where her derringer rested.

"Lugo, it's time. Remember, we don't want the lady dead; we just want her cut . . . the way you handled that drummer back in Denver."

Lugo took a step closer and raised his knife.

Even in the faint light of the alley, Nora could see the

gleam of the blade. With effort, she was barely able to reach the grip of the derringer with her fingertips. She needed to move her hand a little further.

Welker clapped his hand across her mouth again. As he did so, he altered his stance just a bit. It was enough.

Nora could now hold the derringer in her palm. In the instant that she felt the blade of Lugo's knife against her cheek, she fired . . . through the pocket of her coat. She saw Lugo wince as he immediately clutched his side. The shot was not loud, but loud enough to arouse anyone who might be nearby. Welker shoved her to the ground and began to run. Nora looked up in time to see the pair of them disappear down the alley.

Almost at once, she heard footsteps approaching from the street. She turned and was relieved to see Deputy Johnny Orr converging on her, his gun drawn.

"Are you all right, ma'am?" he asked as he knelt down and helped her to her feet.

"I . . . I think so."

"Ed Slattery was guardin' you tonight. I found him a few minutes ago with a knot on his head. I started off in this direction to see if I could pick up your trail. Lucky for you, I overheard the gunshot."

"That was me," Nora replied, holding the derringer in her palm. "I hit one of them."

"Welker and his partner?"

"Yes."

"Did you see which way they went?"

"They turned south at the end of the alley."

Orr raised his gun and fired three shots in the air in rapid succession. "Will you be all right by yourself for a little longer?"

"Yes. Go on."

Orr turned and followed after Welker and Lugo.

Not more than a minute later, Sheriff Logan and a few of the townsmen arrived on the scene. Nora quickly told Logan what had happened. He ordered one of the locals to escort her back to his office while he and the others followed after Deputy Orr.

Nora was shaking, but by the time she reached the sheriff's office she had recovered somewhat. The warm air and a hot cup of coffee helped to settle her nerves. It was not long afterward that she heard a series of shots, followed by a brief silence, and then another volley of shots. Fifteen minutes later, Welker walked into the office, his hands held high over his head. Sheriff Logan was behind him, his gun leveled on Welker. He ushered his prisoner into a cell in the back room. A minute later, two men entered carrying Lugo's limp form. The small man's eyes were open despite a large stain of blood on his chest one shade darker than his red coat. They carried him into the back room as well. A few minutes after that, Deputy Orr came in with Dr. Bailey.

A short while after that, Slattery was helped inside, holding his head as he staggered to a chair.

Sheriff Logan pulled a bottle of whiskey from his desk drawer and filled a glass for him.

Slattery took a long pull and then nodded that he

was all right. "Sorry, Sheriff. I didn't even see anybody comin'."

"It's okay, Ed. Everything worked out just fine. Do you want the doc to take a look at your head?"

"Naw, I'll be all right. The wife's hit me harder than this with her skillet."

Logan chuckled. "Slim, will you see to it that Ed gets home?"

Slim nodded and helped Slattery to his feet.

Logan removed his coat and hung it up. He sat down behind his desk, poured himself a drink, and downed it. "Well, Miss Masters, your playmates are locked up safe and sound."

"Thank goodness."

"We cornered 'em in Barrow's Livery . . . had a nice little shootout. Welker was bad enough but you should've seen Lugo. He was swingin' from the rafters like a regular monkey. He even swept down on us from a rope. I had to put a slug in his chest to stop him, but he should live to stand trial. We found enough cutlery on him to start a mercantile. Every time I searched him I found another knife. I wouldn't be surprised if Doc doesn't find a couple he might've swallowed."

"I can still feel Lugo's knife against my face," Nora said as she touched her cheek.

"They're quite a pair."

"They were determined that Will Grant had stolen the payroll. They figured I could get it for them."

"When Will Grant first put me on to these boys, I sent

off some wires, inquiring about 'em. It seems that they're wanted for questioning in an assault in Denver. Lugo's last name is Karoleon. He worked for the circus. Did a little bit of everything. He was part of a trapeze and high wire act. He was known as the 'Albino Ape.' After that, he graduated to knife throwing. It appears that he got so handy with his knives that he preferred them to people."

Nora shivered. "I think I'll be seeing those two in my nightmares for some time to come."

"You must be done in. I'll have someone see you to your hotel."

Chapter Fourteen

The following morning Sheriff Logan dispatched Johnny Orr to bring Will Grant into town. When they walked into the sheriff's office, Logan and Nora were waiting.

"Good morning, Will," Logan said.

"Morning, Sheriff."

"Hello, Mr. Grant."

"Miss Masters."

"Thanks for coming in," Logan said.

"Your deputy filled me in on what happened last night." Turning to Nora, he said, "I'm mighty sorry to hear about the close shave you had. I'm glad you weren't hurt."

"Thank you. I'm fine."

"Your friends are in a cell, Will. I want you to identify them officially and sign a statement about Karl Tarver's death."

Grant nodded.

"Leave your iron on my desk."

Grant did as he was told and then followed the sheriff into the back room. Lugo was stretched out on a bunk, his chest heavily bandaged. His white hair hung in long, loose strands on his pillow. His colorless eyes were open, affixed on the ceiling in an aimless stare. Welker was sitting on a bunk on the opposite side of the cell, his back against the wall, one knee elevated as he propped his boot on the mattress. His eyes narrowed as he saw Grant enter.

Grant glanced at Logan and nodded. "They're the ones."

Welker got to his feet and slunk over to Grant. He wrapped his fingers around the bars in front of him and sneered. "Well, Will, it looks as though you got away with it after all."

Grant shook his head. "I hate to disappoint you, Joe, but you had it all wrong. The sheriff here is clean, and I never took that money. You had me cornered, and I just concocted that story to get you off my back."

Welker stared at him in disbelief.

"It's the truth, all right. I served time for something I didn't do. You bet all your money on a horse that was scratched at the gate."

Welker's face dropped.

* * *

Grant signed the sheriff's statement and then picked up his gun. "I see that you've got another empty cell, Sheriff. Get ready to fill it."

Logan stared at him curiously.

"I know now who robbed the express office and killed Tom Elsworth."

Logan's back straightened as his eyes locked onto Grant's.

Nora rose to her feet.

"You'll know soon enough. I should be back in town in a couple of hours, and you can make your arrest then."

"A couple of hours?"

"Where are you going, Mr. Grant?" Nora asked.

"I have to break some news to someone first. Then, I'll be back."

"Will, I don't know exactly what you've got in mind but—"

"It won't do you any good to try to talk me out of it. I'm going to do this my way. I've waited a long time for this, and I plan to wipe the books clean—for Tom Elsworth's sake, as well as my own."

Logan folded his arms as he considered Grant. "All right, Will, do what you have to do, but I'll expect you to operate within the law."

"I always have."

"I thought as much," Logan replied, a slight smile on his face.

As Grant left the office, Nora turned to Logan. "What do you think he has in mind?"

Logan rubbed his chin and then shook his head.

Nora stepped outside and watched Grant mount up and ride out of town. She walked over to *The Tribune* and entered the office, where she found Frank Dunbar sitting at her desk. Smiling, he said, "Our inquiries have yielded some interesting information."

Suddenly, Grant felt very tired. It was more than the aftermath from the crack on the head that Karl Tarver had administered. It went beyond the icy treatment of some of the townsmen and the threats from the likes of Joe Welker, who wanted money from him that he did not have. It was what he was about to do that made him heartsick. His ride to the Collins spread would be a long one . . . not in distance, but in effort. He had to dig deep within himself to complete the journey because it was the last thing on earth he wanted to do. He was faced with a strange irony. In a sense, he did not want to reach his destination, yet he could not stop until he did. It was a rotten feeling all the way around. He had never experienced such a sensation within his heart before, but he kept remembering Elsworth, the express office robbery, and his time in prison. It was those memories that empowered him to ride on.

It was a warm, cloudless day, and the sun was high in the sky. There were still pecks of snow on the ground left over from the last winter storm, but Grant had a sense that the back of winter was broken. The bay moved steadily, picking its way around the rock-studded road while Grant sat in the saddle, half intent on direction, half lost in thought. He considered it odd how he tended to notice little things he had never observed before—the way the brush hung over the edge of the road, the trees in the distance, their bare limbs still covered with a layer of snow. Perhaps he was subconsciously attempting to lose himself—to blend in with his surroundings. He shook off the feeling and urged the bay onward, determined to finish what he had started, anxious for the next day to come in the hope that it would be a better one.

He saw the smoke from the chimney of the Collins ranch before he saw the house. It rose slowly in a feathery column before disappearing high into the sky. He knew that Mary was probably cooking or doing housework. He was loath to disturb her, but he knew that he owed her this visit.

Soon, he brought the house in view, and before he realized it, he was at the hitching rail, where he dismounted and tied the bay. Slowly, he made his way onto the porch and knocked. The door opened quickly, and Mary was standing before him. She was wearing a yellow dress with a white lace collar. Her face appeared to be freshly scrubbed, and her hair was neatly combed just off her ears. She beamed brightly when she saw him.

"Why, Will! This is a pleasant surprise. Come in out of the cold."

Grant removed his Stetson and stepped inside, where he was immediately met with the inviting aromas of apples and cinnamon. "Hello, Mary."

"Your head is bandaged. What happened?"

"It's nothing," he replied, shaking off the importance of his injury.

"I just took a pie out of the oven not twenty minutes ago. Why don't I put on some coffee?"

He shook his head. "No thanks . . . not just now."

Mary seemed to sense that something was troubling him. "What is it, Will? Is there something wrong?"

Grant shifted his weight from one foot to the other. "I'm afraid there is. Do you think we could sit down?"

She frowned as she took Grant by the arm and led him to the settee. She sat down, and Grant dropped down heavily beside her. He took her hand in his and squeezed it slightly.

"Mary, I don't know exactly how to tell you this."

"What is it, Will?"

"It's about Steve."

Her eyes widened as her fingers tightened around his hand. "Is he all right?"

"Yes."

"Then what?"

"It's hard for me to tell you this, but I believe that Steve is the man responsible for killing Tom Elsworth and robbing the express office."

Mary stared at him in silence for a long moment. Finally, she released his hand and drew away from him. "Will, what are you saying?"

"I know it's difficult to believe, Mary, but I'm afraid it's true."

"How can you say such a thing about my brother? Steve has always been by your side—all through the trial and now. Why, he's the best friend you have in Coltonville or anywhere for that matter."

"I'm afraid he's deceived you as well, Mary."

Her face reddened as she rose to her feet. "Will, I thought you had feelings for me. How can you come here and make such an accusation?"

Grant stood up. "I'm here because I care for you, Mary. I came here first . . . to break the news to you as painlessly as I could . . . before I confront Steve and before I go to the sheriff. I thought you had the right to know. I didn't want you to hear it from anyone else."

"I can assure you that your suspicions are wrong. Steve could never do anything like that. He could never hurt anyone."

Grant took a deep breath and exhaled slowly. "I've had a long time to think this through, and I know I'm right. Steve was working at the express office the week of the robbery. Tom hired him to add shelving to the storage room. Tom knew Steve and he trusted him. With the payroll there, Tom wouldn't have allowed anyone else near the place. Steve knew that I would be dropping by to pick up Tom, and he knew when I was coming because he overheard our conversation earlier that day. He held Tom at gunpoint until I entered, and then he shot both of us. Whether he wanted to kill me or just wound me . . . I don't know. Either way, his plan worked out fine. It looked like I was in on the robbery and Tom shot me before he went down. One way or the other, I took the blame."

"No, that couldn't be."

"The way I figure it is that Charley Ferris was outside on horseback. Steve got the money to Charley, who rode out of town. Witnesses at the trial claimed that they saw or heard a horseman within seconds after the shots were fired, but nobody could identify him in the dark."

"But that doesn't make sense. How did Steve get out of the express office?"

"He didn't. He stayed behind to place Tom's gun in his hand and to replace my .45 with his own. The scene looked exactly the way he wanted it to look . . . as though Tom and I had shot it out. One of us was dead, and the other might as well have been."

Mary's eyes narrowed. "Even if you consider that Steve could've done such a thing, do you think he would be living here under such modest conditions with so much money at his fingertips?"

"It's my guess that Steve was biding his time. Most likely, he planned to wait a year or two before making his move. He always talked, about California. The law has a long arm, but time and distance improve a man's odds."

Mary began to wring her hands.

"When Charley's confession freed me and I returned to Coltonville, Steve was handed the perfect opportunity. He had framed me once. Why not a second time? He saw to it that some of the payroll money surfaced. Not only that, he made certain that I was the one who passed it.

Steve has been in my house many times. He knows where I keep my cash. It would've been easy for him to slip in and exchange some of the payroll money with my own. I wouldn't have noticed the difference so long as the denominations were the same. When the stolen money started appearing—from my hands—it made me look like a prize fool all over again."

"Will, this is crazy. You don't know what you're saying."

"Not only that, but five hundred dollars from the payroll was planted in my saddlebags."

"Anyone could've done that."

"It was rolled up in a sock. The sock had a very distinct odor to it. It was washed in Marberry's soap."

"A lot of people use Marberry's soap."

Grant frowned. "Not in these parts. I checked with Mr. Morris at the mercantile. You're the only one who orders it."

Mary shook her head in despair as she buried her face in her hands.

Grant took her gently by the shoulders and pulled her to him.

For a long moment, she stood next to him and quivered. Finally, she raised her head and looked at him through tears. "What are you going to do, Will?"

"I have to take Steve in."

She searched his face, desperation written all over her own. "There's no other way?"

"You know there isn't."

She nodded grudgingly.

"He's working at the express office now, isn't he?"

"Yes. You won't hurt him?"

"That will be up to him."

"I'm coming with you. He's my brother." Her eyes pleaded with him.

"All right."

"I'll get my coat."

Grant waited uneasily while Mary stepped into the hallway. When she returned, she was bundled up in a thick wool coat. On her head was a matching cap. Grant opened the door for her, and they stepped out onto the porch.

"I'll go to the barn and saddle your horse for you."

"That won't be necessary."

Grant turned to see Mary a few feet behind him, a derringer in her hand. Stunned, he said, "Mary, don't be foolish."

"I don't plan to be, Will, but you're not going to turn Steve in to the law."

"Do you plan to stop me with that?"

"Let's take a walk."

"A walk?"

"Behind the house . . . up over that hill. There's a cave there. It's hidden behind some thick brush. Nobody knows about it. Steve came across it last year when he was searching for strays."

Grant stared at her in disbelief.

"It will be harder for me if I kill you here. I'll have to

drag your body into the barn until Steve returns. You can live a little longer if you do as I say."

"Mary—"

"What do you say, Will, shall we take one last walk together?"

Suddenly, Grant found himself face to face with someone he did not recognize. Mary's eyes were as cold and lifeless as the snow on the mountains in the distance. Her words were flat and threatening.

"I can't imagine you using your gun on me, but at this point I can't afford to gamble. Take out your .45 and toss it aside."

Grant did as she ordered. "That derringer . . . Charley Ferris was killed with a derringer."

"You don't have to ask. It was me who killed Charley, not Steve."

Stunned by her frankness, he could barely speak. "Why?"

"Charley had a conscience, and he talked too much. He felt guilty about Tom Elsworth and about you. He got weaker every month, drank more, became more un-reliable. It was only a matter of time before he would break. I was surprised he lasted as long as he did."

"You killed Charley to protect Steve?"

She smirked.

"When did you find out that it was Steve who pulled the robbery?"

Her smirk widened. "Find out? It was my plan all along. It was Steve who muffed it when he only wounded you. You were supposed to die the same way as Tom Elsworth. That created some loose ends. I was afraid that something might be discovered during the trial, but everything worked out."

"But you and Steve were always at my side. You wrote to me when I was in prison."

"I had to stay close to you, and you confided in me . . . about your trial, your appeal, your conversations and letters with your lawyer. If by chance anything did come to light, I would've been in a position to do something about it."

"You mean something like Charley Ferris?"

She shrugged. "Charley lived five minutes too long. Otherwise, you'd still be sitting in the penitentiary. Oh, he created another problem for me. Because of him, you were released. Then, you started nosing around, trying to find answers. I was confident you wouldn't learn anything, but there was too much at stake. I took out a little insurance. It was easy making you look guilty by simply exchanging some bills from the payroll with the cash in your drawer. It was rather amusing. You were actually spending the stolen money without even realizing it."

"I suppose you did that as well?"

She nodded. "You were a cinch to handle, Will. Somehow, you put enough of the pieces together but it doesn't matter now."

Grant hung his head.

"That way, Will. Start moving, or so help me, I'll drop you where you stand."

Grant turned and began to walk. He felt numb inside. He moved past the house and started up the hill. As he walked, he attempted to sort through Mary's remarks, still uncertain that they had registered with him. He knew that Mary planned to kill him. She made no attempt to conceal it. He realized that he had to act and act quickly, or he would fall victim to her again. Trudging slowly up the hill, he glanced behind from time to time to determine if he could make a move to overpower her. He saw, however, that she was cautious, hanging well back of him. As it stood, she would have little difficulty in shooting him before he could reach her. It was a fool's bet to think that he could succeed; nevertheless, he had no intention of being drilled like a clay pigeon. He decided that if he were to die, he would go down making his best play. He was nearly halfway up the hill when he formulated a plan. He would drop to one knee and roll back down the hill in the hope of knocking Mary off her feet. Perhaps, if he moved quickly enough, he could take her by surprise and force an errant shot. Deep down, he doubted it, but he would try it nonetheless.

Grant measured his steps against the slope of the hill. Mentally preparing himself for what he imagined would be his last move, he took a deep breath and then acted. He suddenly dropped to the ground and rolled. He heard a shot; his shoulder struck something hard. He came up into a kneeling position and found himself two feet short of Mary, who stood over him, a pained expression on her face. Her hand was empty, and blood dribbled from it as she held it awkwardly. Grant looked down and saw the derringer at Mary's feet. He quickly retrieved it. Glancing off to his right, he saw a man not far away, a gun in his hand. There was a familiar look about him. Beside him stood Nora Masters. As Grant climbed to his feet, Nora and the man moved toward him.

"Are you all right, Will?" Nora asked.

"I think so." Eyeing the man, he said, "Did you fire that shot?"

"I did," the man replied.

"I'm mighty grateful."

"Think nothing of it," he said with a grin.

"Will, you remember Frank, don't you?"

"I'm the man you threw out of your house."

Grant nodded. "I remember. Frank Dunbar, isn't it?"

"That's right."

"Well, I guess maybe I had you figured wrong."

Dunbar chuckled. "No, you acted exactly the way I hoped you would. I've been on your case for quite a while now, and I never suspected you of being guilty."

Grant stared at him quizzically. "My case?"

"Frank is a Pinkerton agent."

"A Pinkerton?"

"And so am I," Nora announced.

Grant pushed back his Stetson. "I don't know what to say."

Nora stepped forward, removed a handkerchief from her pocket, and wrapped it around Mary's hand. "We've been assigned to you by the head office. You never behaved like a guilty man, but we had a strong suspicion that you would lead us somewhere, and you did. We got a break when our operatives in St. Louis finally learned the identity of Adele Ferris' cousin . . . Steve Collins."

Grant nodded his understanding.

"And there's something more that you should know." Turning to Mary, she said, "Do you want to tell him, or shall I?"

Mary swore at her through clenched teeth.

Nora smiled. "Mary isn't Steve's sister. She's his wife."

Grant took a deep breath and released it heavily. He regarded Mary once again and shook his head. "Looks like I've been blind to a lot of things."

Nora's lips tightened sympathetically. "Yes, but you've done a pretty good job of tying up the loose ends."

"Speaking of loose ends, there's one more piece of business I have to tend to. It's time I balanced the scales for Tom Elsworth as well as for myself." Turning to Dunbar, he said, "Mind if I borrow your gun?"

"No need to. I've got yours right here," Dunbar replied, pulling Grant's .45 out from under his belt and handing it over.

"I have to ride into town," Grant said as he returned his gun to his holster.

Nora and Dunbar looked at each other.

"I'll get Mary's hand fixed up, and then Frank and I will take her in to the sheriff."

He nodded. "Thanks. I'll be talking to you."

"Be careful, Will," Nora said, and she meant it.

Chapter Fifteen

It was late afternoon when Grant rode back into Coltonville. He guided the bay to a hitching rail on the opposite side of the street from the express office. Dismounting, he tied down the horse and stood in the street. It was not much more than a year ago when he stood on this very spot. He remembered it as if it were yesterday. He was on his way to meet Tom Elsworth for a quiet dinner. It was that night that changed his life forever. He could still see Tom standing behind the counter—just before he was shot and killed. He remembered waking up, wounded, in the sheriff's office. He remembered the looks from the townsmen, the accusations, the trial . . . prison. It had been a nightmare like nothing he could have ever imagined until, that is, he learned the full truth about Mary and Steve. The events . . . the memories . . .

167

had burned him like a brand. Now, it was time to turn the last page and try to put it all behind him. There was but one final detail that required his attention.

Grant slowly unbuttoned his coat. He removed the .45 from his holster and checked the chambers. He returned the gun and then stripped off his coat, which he draped over the hitching rail. Cupping his hand to his mouth, he yelled out, "Collins! Steve Collins!"

There was no response.

"It's over, Steve. Mary's talked. She's in custody. I know everything. I know that you murdered Tom and robbed the express office. Now, I aim to take you in."

There were several townsmen moving about the street or standing on the boardwalk. They stopped what they were doing when they heard Grant. Some of them stared at him; others looked in the direction of the express office.

"Come out, Steve," Grant called.

There was still no response from within the express office.

Grant started to cross the street.

The residents quickly stepped indoors or moved to the end of the block, where they took cover behind buildings or barrels.

"Hold it right there!"

Grant turned to see Sheriff Logan striding up to him. His deputy was trailing behind.

"What do you plan to do, Will?"

"Steve Collins is the man behind the robbery of the express office and the murder of Tom Elsworth."

"Can you prove that?"

"I can."

Logan regarded him closely. "In that case, I'll bring him in." Turning to his deputy, he said, "Johnny, cover the back door."

The young deputy drew his gun and hastened down the alley that flanked the express office.

"This is my play, Sheriff. I called him out."

"I'm still the law here, and I make the arrests."

The men locked eyes for a long moment. Finally, Grant said, "All right, you can make it official if you want, but I'll be walking through that door with you."

"That's fair enough."

Suddenly, a shot exploded from a window of the express office, striking Logan, knocking him to the ground.

Grant pulled his .45 and returned fire. His bullet struck the window sash, but the shutters were quickly shut from within. He knelt down beside Logan and rolled him over. The coat sleeve on the sheriff's left arm had a hole in it, and there was blood leaking out of the hole.

"I'll get you to the doctor," Grant said.

"No. I'm all right. Just get me to my feet."

Grant took hold of Logan's good arm and braced him as the lawman struggled to his feet. He continued to support Logan until he recovered his balance.

The sheriff took a deep breath and then nodded. He

drew his .45, and the two men advanced together toward the express office. When they reached the boardwalk, they took up positions on either side of the front door.

"Come on out, Collins. There's nowhere for you to go," Logan shouted.

They were greeted by silence from within.

Logan motioned for Grant to try the door.

Grant knelt down and reached for the knob. He tried to turn it but the lock was in place. Hastily, he pulled back.

Logan cocked his .45 and fired two rounds into the lock.

Grant then moved in front of the door and kicked it in. The woodwork splintered as the door flung inward, banging against the inside wall. He burst into the office, his gun ready, and Logan came through right after him. They shot quick glances around the room but saw no one. Cautiously, Grant maneuvered his way around the counter, but there was no sign of Steve. Turning their attention to the storage room, they stood with their backs to the wall and eased their way toward the curtains that covered the doorway. Logan parted them with his .45 and peeked through. He shook his head. "There are some small boxes in there and a few large crates. He could be behind any of 'em."

"I don't think so," Grant replied.

Logan glanced at him curiously.

Suddenly, Grant walked through the curtains.

"Will, be careful!"

Disregarding Logan's words, he moved ahead, passing among the crates until he reached the far side of the room.

"Will, what are you doing?" Logan stressed, almost pleading for caution as he trailed behind Grant, glancing nervously from left to right as he maneuvered his way through the storage room.

Grant paid him no heed, moving deliberately until he stood just a few feet from the wall on the far side of the room.

"Here!" Logan exclaimed, pausing to pick up a Winchester that lay on the floor. Sniffing the weapon, he announced, "This gun's been fired." A look at the back door told him that it was barred from inside. He stepped over to the only window in the storage room, which faced onto the back alley. The shutters were ajar. "He must've climbed out this way." Flinging open the shutters, he peered outside. "Johnny!"

In a moment, they heard the deputy's voice.

"Johnny, did Collins come out this window?"

"No, sir. I've got the back door and the window covered. Nobody's come out."

"That can't be," Logan stated in disbelief. "He didn't get by us. He didn't disappear into thin air." His eyes drifted back over the larger containers. "Maybe he's inside one of the crates."

"I don't think so."

Logan eyed Grant inquisitively.

"It was exactly like this a year ago . . . when you found me here . . . unconscious. You said that no one had left the office by the front door. The rear door and the windows were barred. I was the only one here."

"But this time we know that Collins was here. He shot at us from the window."

Grant nodded. "Collins was here then too."

"You're not making any sense. Somehow, he's slipped past us. I'll form a posse."

Grant placed his hand on Logan's chest and held him in place. Then, he took a step closer toward the far wall.

Logan followed Grant's line of sight. The far wall was about ten feet long. It was lined with shelves, on which rested an assortment of small boxes, parcels, and other supplies. He watched as Grant paced back and forth in front of the shelves, looking up and down, until his eyes finally settled on something on the floor. Then, Grant knelt down and examined something in one corner of the room. When he appeared satisfied, a small grin formed on his face, and he stepped away from the shelves. He turned toward Logan, wearing an inexplicable expression.

Logan was about to speak when Grant faced the shelves again and said, "You can come out now, Steve. Come out while you can."

Logan stared at him quizzically.

After a pause, Grant raised his .45. Training it on the shelves, just above eye level, he fired. The sound of the gun discharging in such a confined space was deafening. Ten seconds later, Grant fired again and again. He then took the rifle from Logan's hand and levered in a shell. "I'll empty the Winchester if I have to, Steve . . .

and I'll keep aiming lower and lower . . . and if that doesn't do the job, I'll burn this building to ashes."

"Will, what the—"

Logan's words were interrupted by a muffled response. There was a slight noise, followed by a scraping sound. Some of the packages on the shelves began to shake as a section of the wall began to move. A seam appeared and half of the wall separated from the other half.

"Don't shoot! I give up! I'm not armed," Collins' voice called from out of nowhere. He suddenly emerged from behind the shelves, his eyes wide, his face pale as he held both of his hands in the air.

Logan eyed him for a long moment before a sense of realization set in. He then removed a set of manacles from his belt and handed them to Grant. "You want to do the honors?"

"You bet I do," Grant replied as he placed the restraints on Collins' wrists.

"Almost all the money's there. I didn't touch it until Will got out of prison. It never left the express office," Collins announced, his lips trembling nervously.

Logan pushed by Collins and examined the recess behind the wall of shelves. "There's a space here—not more than two feet deep. These shelves seem to be on hinges. There's a pouch here." Logan opened it and looked inside. "Money . . . and plenty of it."

Grant nodded.

Logan stepped over to the window. "Johnny! Get in here!"

Thirty seconds later, the deputy rushed in.

Logan leveled his eyes on Collins. "Steve Collins, I arrest you for the robbery of the express office and the murder of Tom Elsworth."

Collins hung his head.

"Deputy, take this vermin to jail and don't let him out of your sight."

"Yes, sir," Orr replied, taking Collins by the arm and leading him off.

Inspecting the hidden recess more closely, Logan said, "He's a clever devil, that one."

"It explains a lot, Sheriff."

"That it does. He was here all the time when we searched the office on the night of the robbery. He probably slipped out in the middle of the night . . . after everyone left . . . and no one was any the wiser."

"Steve wasn't in it alone, Sheriff. His wife played a hand as well."

"His wife?"

"That's right. Mary isn't his sister."

Logan frowned as he pushed back his Stetson. "There are still plenty of questions, but by everything I hold sacred, before I'm through, I'll have the answer to every one of 'em."

"There's plenty of time for answers. I did my share of waiting. I'm not in any hurry anymore."

"It looks like this town owes you an apology . . . and this lawman does as well." He extended his hand.

Grant took it.

Chapter Sixteen

Grant arose late the next morning. Still, he felt tired. He washed and shaved. As he looked in the mirror, he thought that his face appeared haggard. He dressed slowly, made his bed, and then drifted into the kitchen where he made coffee.

He heard a horse approaching, and he immediately lifted his .45 from its holster. Moving to the window, he recognized Sheriff Logan. He shook his head and thought that it was a sad commentary when a man had to arm himself to greet a visitor. He replaced the weapon and went to the door. He found the air cold outside as he waited for Logan to tie his horse. He saw that the left sleeve of the sheriff's coat was empty, and the lawman moved a bit awkwardly as he stepped onto the porch.

"Mornin', Will."

175

"Come in, Sheriff."

Logan removed his Stetson and hung it on a peg near the door. He unbuttoned his sheepskin coat, revealing a sling that supported his arm.

"How's the wing?"

"Not bad. The doc says I should stay in bed another day but I've got things to do."

"Sit down. I just made some coffee."

"I could use some to take the chill off the mornin' air. I reckon we're mostly done with the snow, but the cold will linger on for a spell."

Grant filled a cup and placed it in front of the sheriff. "You didn't ride all the way out here to discuss the weather."

Logan took a sip of the hot liquid and shook his head. "No, I didn't. I've been questioning Steve Collins and his . . . wife, Mary. She's as close as a clam, but Steve's surrendered himself to hard reality. He's been spillin' his guts."

Grant swirled the coffee in his cup and regarded Logan with interest.

"It was Mary who first got the idea of robbing the express office, all right, but it was Steve who actually carried it out. It came to him when he was hired by Tom Elsworth to make repairs and add shelves in the back room. Steve is an excellent carpenter. It was a simple enough task for him to construct a false wall as he did, concealed behind the shelves. It was nothing but a storage room—dark most of the time—and it would take a keen eye for someone to notice such a small change. Tom certainly wouldn't have noticed it, not at the time anyway, concerned as he was with guardin' the payroll.

"On the day of the robbery, Steve finished his work on the false wall. Before leaving, however, he unbarred the shutters over the window in the storage room. He took his tools and said good night to Tom, who let him out through the front door, locking it afterward. In fact, Steve said that he heard Tom secure the lock before he stepped off the boardwalk. Steve then slipped down the alley, moved to the rear of the express office, and entered through the window. He then barred the shutters from the inside and waited in the dark. Through an earlier conversation with Tom, Steve knew that you were coming by at six o'clock. Not long before six, he threw down on Tom and forced him to open the safe. He then held Tom at gunpoint until you arrived. After that . . . well, you know the story."

Grant nodded.

Logan took a swallow of coffee. "I asked Steve if he fired at you with the intent to wound you or to kill you."

Grant eyed him closely.

"He didn't answer."

"Maybe he doesn't know the answer himself. Likely as not, we never will."

Logan shrugged. "Steve figured it would be too risky to attempt an escape after he fired the shots. There would be too many descending on the express office. He simply retreated into the back room and concealed himself behind the wall he had constructed. He was there all the time while my deputy and I searched the storage room. The back door and every window in the express office were barred. We could only assume that the thief had left by the front door, which was unlocked."

"And Charley was waiting outside on horseback—the one that witnesses heard galloping away in the dark."

"That's right. Charley was Steve's cousin. He was at the Collins house the night they planned the robbery. He was drunk, and they thought he was asleep, but he overheard them plotting the whole thing. He demanded that he be cut in. They had no choice but to agree. Mary had planned to play the role, but Charley took it on instead. His job was simple—to ride off as soon as he heard the shots. Everyone naturally thought that there were two holdup men. One was shot and left behind. That was you. The other got away with the payroll. There wasn't much risk in it for Charley. With the head start he had, there wasn't much chance in catching him at night, and no one did. Even if he was caught, he could always claim ignorance of the entire matter. He wasn't carrying the payroll. He wasn't even armed. Anyone on his trail would most likely assume that there must've been another rider. After all, who would ever think that the town drunk had pulled off such a crime?"

"I didn't. Sitting on my bunk in my prison cell, I found it hard to swallow that Charley Ferris was involved."

"You can understand why so many of the locals questioned your release."

Grant nodded.

"Steve then slipped out later that night—after all the activity had died down. Not long afterward, he got a job working at the express office. Tom had recommended him for it. For that reason, there was no point in even moving the money. Steve had access to it any time he needed it, but he had planned to sit on it for a full year before he and Mary touched any of it. The trail would've been colder by then."

"Steve always talked about going to California. Nobody would've thought anything of it if he finally left. It would've been easier to get rid of the money along the way."

Logan nodded in agreement. "But Charley started to fall apart. He never felt right about letting you take the blame and rot in prison. Steve got him out of town, sent him to Ridley, but he continued to drink more and more. When he finally broke down completely and threatened to talk, they killed him. Unfortunately for them, he didn't die right away. It was his confession that got you released from prison."

"Mary admitted to me yesterday that she did the shooting."

"Steve wouldn't comment on that."

"I suppose it doesn't really matter now one way or the other."

Logan eyed him closely. "She meant a great deal to you, didn't she?"

"She did. She wrote to me while I was in prison . . .

she kept up my house . . . but it was all for the wrong reasons. How could I have been so wrong?"

"There are those who claim that the betrayal of a friend is the worst crime of all."

Grant leaned forward, folded his hands on the table, and hung his head.

Logan took a long swallow of coffee before he spoke again. "Charley's daughter, Adele, came west with the intention of visiting her father's grave. Before she left, she wrote to Steve, hoping to visit him as well. He knew when she would be arriving. For obvious reasons, he couldn't have her showing up here in town or even in Ridley. Her visit would've revealed the relationship between Steve and Charley, and that could've led to some uncomfortable questions. Steve intercepted the stage carrying Adele and killed her and the driver before they reached their destination, trying to make it look like a robbery."

Grant shook his head in disdain. "It's all a little ironic—the killing of so many people over a pouch of money—money that was never really spent. Ruined lives, bitterness, regret . . . for what?"

"I've been a lawman for better than twenty years. I still see things that I can't explain. There's no tellin' what some folks will do for greed or women or even power. Steve Collins always seemed like a decent sort. When he started down this road, I doubt that he knew what direction it would take him."

"No, I don't imagine anyone could've guessed how

far this has gone. Mary was someone I thought I could build a future with. Steve was a man I trusted."

Logan nodded his understanding as his hand drifted toward his sling. He passed his fingers over his arm as he stared at an invisible spot on the table.

"Your arm giving you some trouble?"

"Oh . . . a little, I guess. It's just a nuisance more than anything."

"More coffee?"

"No, I'd best be goin'." He hesitated. "Oh, I nearly forgot the main reason I dropped by. When the payroll was stolen last year, the head office offered a reward for its return. That reward still stands, and it rightly belongs to you. You're the one who truly found it."

Grant shook his head. "As far as I'm concerned, it's blood money, Sheriff. There would be too many bad memories associated with it."

"I understand how you feel, Will, but money is money. Besides, I reckon that most folks in town would feel better if you got something back after all that's happened to you."

Grant shrugged.

"Think it over. It'll take a few days for me to arrange for a pay authorization. After that, it's yours if you want it. It would be nice if something good came out of this."

As Logan pushed himself away from the table, Grant asked, "By the way, did you know that Miss Masters was a Pinkerton?"

"Yep. She and her partner contacted me shortly after

their arrival in Coltonville. I had a strong feelin' from the beginning that she believed in you. She thought that you deserved a chance to prove your innocence, and she was willin' to help. She's quite a woman, that one. I'll be on my way now. I just thought you'd want to know all the facts."

"Thanks, Sheriff."

Chapter Seventeen

Two days later, Grant was sitting in the cafe over breakfast. He was rested, his mind was clear, and he felt better in every regard. The latest edition of *The Tribune* was spread out in front of him, and he was reading through Nora Masters' column for the second time. He was surprised when he looked up and saw her standing at his table.

"Hello, Will. I see that you're reading my column."

"As a matter of fact, I am."

"What do you think?"

He stood and pulled out a chair for her. She sat down and unbuttoned her coat. Her brown eyes were wide, and her face looked fresh and a bit red from the sting of the morning cold. The burn of the sun gave her complexion a nice glow and created a pleasant harmony with her auburn hair. She wore a green dress with a cameo brooch at her neck.

"Would you like some breakfast?"

"Oh, I've already eaten, but some coffee would be nice."

He signaled the waitress to bring another cup.

"The column—what do you think?" she asked as she removed her gloves.

"Well, you've certainly got all the facts straight."

She seemed pleased.

"You've gone to great lengths to make the town feel guilty for convicting me in the first place."

"The town was wrong to convict you. Whenever a man goes to prison for something he hasn't done, a miscarriage of justice has been committed."

Grant shrugged. "It's over and done with. I no longer harbor any grudges. I had a fair trial, and you have to admit—the circumstances were unusual."

She shook her head. "I knew from the first time we met that you weren't the kind of man who could commit a robbery, much less kill a man. Hopefully, this article will set the record straight between you and this town."

"Oh, I think it's already done that. One person has already referred to me as 'sir,' and a member of the jury that convicted me approached me and apologized."

She beamed. "Well! Then my writing has had a positive influence after all."

"I guess you can say that."

She sipped her coffee. "What else do you think . . . about the newspaper column, I mean?"

"Well, you did get a little flowery at one point or two."

Her smile vanished. "Flowery? I don't understand."

"This description of me, for example . . . 'Will Grant, a handsome young rancher whose inner strength enabled him to endure a grave injustice . . . ' " he read from the newspaper.

"Well, it's true." She averted him with her eyes. "You are handsome."

"Yes, I know. I was referring to the part about the 'inner strength.' "

Looking up, she found him smiling at her. "Oh, you're just teasing me."

"Actually, I am. The truth is that you did a very professional job. It's hard to believe that you're a Pinkerton agent and not a real reporter."

She nodded, obviously touched by his remark. "Thank you. I'd be dishonest if I said I wasn't seeking your approval. After all, no one knows the ins and outs of this case better than you."

"You've done an accurate job of reporting, and you've shown a style all your own."

"You don't know how much your words mean to me. I've always wanted to be a reporter. Ever since I've taken on this assignment of working undercover in a newspaper office, I've been doing some serious thinking about leaving the agency. I've spoken to Mr. Creighton about my situation, and he has agreed to keep me on if I choose. He says that, with time and hard work, I can be good enough to make a profession from my writing."

"He ought to know."

"Of course, it won't be right away. I'll have to return to the city, file my report. I'll discuss the matter with my superiors, make the necessary arrangements."

Deep inside, Grant felt excited about her announcement. He had already admitted to himself that he was attracted to her. He liked having her around. He enjoyed talking to her, looking at her, being with her. "I hope it won't take too long," he replied.

Nora stared at him, wide-eyed. She picked up her gloves and turned them over nervously in her hands.

"I was thinking of asking you to dinner. Will you have time before you leave?"

"Yes, and I would like very much to have dinner with you."

He reached across the table and held her hands in his. "Thanks for everything."

She smiled at him and nodded.

"I'll walk you out."

He took her arm as they left the cafe.